Room for Magic

Annika Stone

Room for Magic

Prologue

Sarah Porter had climbed these stairs every night for sixty years, but tonight, her hip protested each step as if the inn itself was trying to hold her back. The September wind rattled the windows in their frames, carrying the scent of dying leaves and distant woodsmoke, autumn's first real announcement that summer's reign had ended.

"Not yet, old friend," she murmured, gripping the mahogany banister worn smooth by countless hands. "One more thing to do."

The Starlight Arbor Inn's Stargazer Suite waited at the top of the turret, three stories up. She could have taken the narrow elevator, installed twenty years ago when her knees first began complaining, but tonight called for the stairs. Some conversations required effort, the kind that left you breathless and certain. The lynx had always preferred those who took the harder path.

Each step brought memories: Ella at five, unafraid, racing up these same stairs in her nightgown, convinced she'd heard the lynx padding through the halls. The child had been right, of course. Children always knew the truth about this place before logic taught them otherwise.

The brass key in her palm had warmed to her touch, though she suspected she wouldn't need it. She was right. As her feet found the third-floor landing, the turret room's door swung open with a soft sigh, like a child greeting a beloved grandmother.

"Hello to you too," Sarah said, stepping inside.

The constellation ceiling glowed without electricity, stars mapping themselves across the domed surface, sometimes in patterns no astronomer would recognize. These were the inn's stars, the ones that had guided lovers together for over a century. There—the Lynx constellation, seven stars forming the shape of a prowling cat. A pattern that, once recognized, could be see all over Green Arbor.

The air smelled of night-blooming jasmine. Impossible, as the last of the summer blooms had faded weeks ago. But the inn had never been constrained by ordinary seasons.

Through the curved windows, Lake Michigan

stretched endless and dark, its surface rippling with starlight. To the west, she could just make out the decommissioned lighthouse, dark now but waiting. It hadn't lit for a true love match in three years, not since the Hendersons' boy had met his wife in the Lighthouse Keeper's Room.

Sarah had a feeling that would change soon.

Her knees protested as she lowered herself to the padded canvas window seat, but she managed it with the same determination that had carried her through six decades of wayward travelers' mishaps and midnight emergencies. She pulled up a corner of the padding. Her fingers found the hidden catch in the wood paneling just underneath the seat, revealing a drawer that shouldn't have existed in such a shallow space.

From the pocket of her decadently plush bathrobe—Harry's last Christmas gift, worn soft with love—she withdrew three items. First, a letter sealed with burgundy wax and pressed with a star—the same seal her own grandmother had used. *For Ella* was written across the front in Sarah's careful script.

Next, a leather journal worn soft with age, its pages filled with three generations of Thompson women's observations about the inn's peculiar ways. The margins held pressed flowers that still held their color, sketches of lynx paw prints that appeared in the morning dew, notes about which rooms helped heal hearts and which ones revealed truth.

Last, a small brass key on a charm shaped like a star, still warm though it had been tucked in her jewelry box for decades—the key to the tea room's secret cabinet, where the real magic lived.

"She'll need these," Sarah told the room. "Though knowing Ella, she'll try to logic her way through everything first. Gets that from her mother's side."

The walls creaked gently. What she like to think of as the inn's version of fond laughter. A warm draft swirled through the room despite the closed windows, ruffling the pages of the journal until it fell open to a pressed forget-me-not, still vivid blue. Liam Carter, age seven, had given her that flower, solemn as a judge. "For your collection, Mrs. Porter. Grandpa says the inn likes flowers."

That boy understood. As for his grandfather, well...

Sarah set the three items in the drawer, slid it closed, patted it, and made her slow way back to the door.

Each room she passed on her descent seemed to bid farewell in its own way. The Rose Suite released a phantom breath of heirloom roses, petals that had witnessed a thousand first kisses. The Lighthouse Room's doorknob glowed faintly, a beacon in the dim hallway, pulsing with the rhythm of a heartbeat waiting to quicken. The Blue Room's door stood slightly ajar, revealing a shaft of impossible golden light. Dawn was still hours away, but the room had its own relationship with time.

From somewhere deep in the walls came a soft chiming, like wine glasses touched in a distant toast.

Downstairs, the lobby waited in midnight shadows, moonlight streaming through the tall windows and painting everything in silver and secrets. The dark hardwood floors, polished by her own hands more times than she could count, reflected the light like still water. On its pedestal by the front desk, where it had stood for over a century, sat the pride of the inn, its giant, one-of-a-kind sand globe.

In the moonlight, the glass seemed to pulse with inner light. The golden sand along the bottom quarter of the globe lay still as held breath, but she could sense the energy coiled within, waiting. The tiny lynx figure sat perched on its dune, those golden gemstone eyes watching, always watching. Waiting.

She placed both palms on the carved old oak base, feeling the subtle vibration that always lived in the wood. The same frequency as a cat's purr, as the earth's own heartbeat.

"She's coming home, isn't she?"

The globe erupted.

Golden-blond sand funneled into a cloud within the glass, forming shapes as it spun with gentle purpose. A lynx prowling through dune grass, ears alert for whispers on the wind. Two figures dancing—no, not dancing. Sarah looked closer. They were working together, the woman's curls escaping from her bun as she reached for something, the man's broad shoulders bending to help her, their hands meeting over what looked like... a coffee pot?

The sand swirled again, showing stars falling like snow, the lighthouse beam sweeping across water, roses blooming in fast-forward, and finally—the lynx again, but not alone. Two cubs played at its feet while it stood guard, watching over something precious just beyond the frame.

In sixty years, Sarah had seen it swirl without prompting only a handful of times—the night she'd arrived, young and widowed and terrified. The morning she'd met Harry at the market. The day Ella was born.

She pressed her forehead to the cool glass.

Let it be true.

Sarah touched the star pendant at her throat, another Thompson heirloom. She'd be glad to see Harry again.

So glad.

A light from the tea room glowed the softest white. Sarah knew she'd turned off all the lights, and certainly wouldn't have missed any of the hobnail glass hurricane lamps. She made her way there, behind the lobby and to the right. Mrs. Frankl was preparing tea, the steam rising in curious spirals.

"Mei-Lin," Sarah said, entering. "You didn't have to—"

"Passages and Promises?" the inn's housekeeper interrupted, naming the blend she was preparing. "The lynx's own recipe, passed down from keeper to keeper. We've done this before, Sarah Porter. I know my role."

Sarah had never gotten a straight answer to why the inn was no longer called The Lynx. Especially since half the town still called it that.

The tea room wrapped around them like an embrace, every surface worn smooth by countless hands seeking comfort, community, or just another cookie. The air hummed with the memory of whispered confessions and celebrated joys, first dates and final farewells.

They sat in comfortable silence at one of the dark waxed-wood tables for guests, the matching chairs with straw-woven seats creaking only the slightest bit. As the tea steeped, the blend filled the room with notes of jasmine and something indefinable—hope, perhaps, or the promise of dawn after a long night.

For a moment, Sarah could swear she heard it: a whisper on the wind that sounded like her grandmother's voice, and her grandmother's grandmother's, all the way back to the first woman who'd stood in this garden and made a bargain with something wild and protective and eternal.

Love protects this land.

"You could have told Ella years ago," Mrs. Frankl said finally.

"She had to choose to come back." Sarah accepted her cup, the warmth seeping into her stiff fingers. "She needed to try the city, to build something of her own first. Now she'll understand what she's choosing."

"And if she doesn't stay?"

Sarah smiled into her tea, tasting future in the jasmine steam. "She will. The Thompson women always do. Eventually."

"Stubborn," Mrs. Frankl muttered. "Every one of you."

"Pot, meet kettle," Sarah replied.

The clock chimed three—the witching hour, Harry used to call it. Time for promises and revelations.

"Watch over her, Mei-Lin. She'll be prickly at first."

"Like her grandmother was." Mrs. Frankl's stern face softened. "Twenty-five years old, crying in my kitchen because the coffee pot was wrong and three couples had been accidentally booked into the same room."

"I was so young. Thank the stars you were there to help me."

"As I'll help her." Mrs. Frankl reached across the

table, squeezing Sarah's hand. "The inn knows its own, Sarah. It won't let her fail."

As Sarah made her way back through the sleeping inn, each step on the old floors sang a different note, a lifetime's worth of footfalls remembered in wood and whisper.

Her own suite on the two lower floors the turret welcomed her with familiar warmth. Harry's presence lingered here strongest, in the indent on his side of the bed, in the coffee mug he'd left on the windowsill that she'd never had the heart to move. She'd finally put a little loam and a peony in there, so Mei-Lin would stop trying to "clean it up" and take it away.

She moved through the rooms one last time, touching memories. The desk where she'd balanced the books, first in giant ledgers and now on spreadsheets. The window where she'd watched countless sunsets paint the lake silver. Upstairs, the bed where Harry had held her through grief and joy and all the ordinary days between.

Her small suitcase waited by the door, packed for the hospital. But first, she draped her cardigan—soft grey wool that smelled perpetually of lilacs and cinnamon— over her office chair. Ella would need it. The nights could get cold until you discovered their secrets.

She pulled one last thing from her pocket: a photograph, edges soft with handling. Ella at eleven or twelve, her last summer here, standing in the garden with dirt on her nose and triumph in her eyes, holding the biggest tomato the heritage plants had ever produced. Liam Carter, lanky at nineteen and trying so hard to look like he hadn't been watching her, caught right at the edge of the frame.

She tucked it into the cardigan pocket. Let Ella find it when she was ready to remember.

Pressing her palm to the wall, she felt the inn's heartbeat through wood and plaster—strong, steady, eternal. "Take care of her. She'll need you more than I did. She's been away too long."

The inn settled around her, creaks and sighs that sounded like a lullaby. Or a promise.

Dawn came softly, autumn sun painting the lake in shades of copper and gold, the water still holding summer's warmth but promising winter's chill. Her back to the morning mist over the hill behind her Sarah sat in her wooden rocking chair on the front porch, watching light chase shadows from the dunes and the bluff and the water. Tracing the suggestion of paw prints —maybe bear, maybe lynx, maybe nothing—that led from the dunes to the front door and back again.

A taxi rolled up the drive, unusually early. Jim Pearson stepped out, hat in hand. "Hospital, Mrs. Porter, ma'am?"

"Yes, Jim. It's time."

As if summoned by her words, they appeared: Agnes, Beatrice, and Cordelia emerging from the morning mist like the Fates themselves, though none were scheduled to work. They wore their best house-dresses, faces solemn with the weight of transition. Mrs. Frankl emerged from the tea room, wiping her hands on her apron.

"No changes until she asks for them," Sarah told the sisters. "The special tea recipes are in the usual place," she reminded Mrs. Frankl.

To the inn itself, she whispered, "Please. Be patient."

As the taxi pulled away, Sarah allowed herself one look back. Every window in the inn caught the sunrise simultaneously, turning the building into a prism of light. Through the front window, she thought she could se the sand globe swirling gently, like a hand waving goodbye.

Or hello.

Chapter One

Six weeks later

The check engine light had been glowing since Benzonia, but Ella Thompson figured if her thirdhand Ford Focus had made it this far, it could limp the last thirty miles to Green Arbor.

She gripped the steering wheel tighter as the two-lane highway twisted through northern Michigan like a ribbon tossed by a careless hand. It was the kind of road she hadn't traveled in years—no stoplights, no cell towers, no billboards promising anything except the occasional scenic overlook. Just trees beginning their autumn show, the mysterious "Whispering Lynx Trail - Next Left," and glimpses of Lake Michigan through the turning leaves like a promise she wasn't ready to keep.

Home. The word sat uneasily in her chest, shifting with each curve of the road. Chicago was home. Her studio apartment with its view of exactly one tree and half a Starbucks sign was home. The Starlight Arbor Inn was... what? A summer memory? A responsibility she'd inherited along with her grandmother's pearl necklace and seventeen years of guilt?

Nobody even told her or mom about the funeral. Not invited. Then again, after what Mom had said all those years ago, everyone probably assumed she wouldn't want to go.

But then the lawyer came a week later, and said Gran gave most everything to Ella. How did that make any sense?

Her metal coffee tumbler rattled in the cup holder—evidence of her pre-dawn escape from the city. A venti monstrosity that had been filled three times today, it bore lipstick marks in "Confidence Red," the shade she'd worn to the meeting to pitch her great new business proposal yesterday. As if the right lipstick could make pitching adding a new boutique hotel to their chain sight unseen go any better.

"Get out, Thompson," her boss had said, typically direct. "Come back when you have facts, numbers. You know, a real proposal."

So here she was, blowing her two weeks of saved vacation time to drive up to her estranged family's probably dilapidated, possibly haunted inn. Super rational life choice.

The radio crackled, losing the classic rock station she'd been clinging to since Milwaukee. Static filled the car, then cleared into something else entirely. "Dream a little dream of me..."

Ella's hands tightened on the wheel.

Grandma Sarah's favorite.

Coincidence.

As the road curved, Lake Michigan revealed itself in full autumn glory. The late afternoon sun turned the water into hammered copper, nothing like the glimpses of gray she caught between Chicago's towers. This was the lake of her childhood—wild and vast, whispering secrets to anybody who took the time to listen. The sight of it made her throat tight in a way she didn't want to examine.

The scent hit her even through the closed windows: pine and earth and that particular mixture of dying leaves and wood smoke that meant autumn in the north. It wrapped around her like her grandmother's hugs, the ones that always bathed her in cinnamon and Chanel No. 5.

Green Arbor materialized as she crested the final hill, unfolding like pages from a scrapbook she'd tried to forget. Main Street stretched below, caught between summer's death and winter's birth. The shops she remembered—Mama Lynx Creamery, Harbor & Home Hardware—sat alongside newcomers trying to look like they'd always belonged. Someone had strung white lights between the lampposts, a little saggy here at the end of summer tourist season.

But before she reached it, the inn's driveway appeared on her left, marked by the same wooden sign she remembered, though the paint looked fresh. Starlight Arbor Inn - Where Love Finds Its Home.

She could have sworn it used to say something else.

The gravel drive curved up sharply, steeper than memory suggested. When she reached the crest, her foot lifted off the gas involuntarily.

There it was.

The inn commanded its hill like a Victorian dowager who refused to acknowledge the passage of time. Three stories of architectural opinion painted in sage and cream, the wide wraparound porch dressed in late-season flowers that had no business blooming this gloriously in September. The single turret rose from the southwest corner with fairy-tale confidence, its windows catching the light like eyes opening after a long sleep.

Definitely not dilapidated.

"You're just a building," Ella whispered, but her hands shook as she pulled into the spot at the far end of the narrow parking lot marked Reserved - Owner. The sign looked new, its paint barely dry.

Her car died with a shudder and a wheeze that suggested it had opinions about her life choices too.

She sat for a moment, watching the inn. The late afternoon light painted everything gold—the weather-vane shaped like a star, the gingerbread trim that looked like lace against the sky, the gardens that someone had been maintaining despite... despite everything.

A breeze stirred, carrying the impossible scent of lilacs. But lilacs bloomed in spring, not September. Unless...

"Unless nothing." She grabbed her purse, fingers brushing the familiar shape of her sketchbook tucked inside—a habit she'd held onto through six years of the corporate grind. "You're exhausted. You're seeing things. You're talking to yourself in a parked car."

Her reflection in the side mirror showed exactly what she expected: chestnut curls escaping from this morning's attempt at a professional bun, hazel eyes shadowed with weariness and something else. Fear? Anticipation? The constellation of freckles across her nose that no amount of concealer had ever hidden stood out pale against her city pallor.

"Right. Professional assessment. Document every-thing." She pulled her phone off its holder next to the coffee cup and pushed open the door. Start with a wide shot, the whole wedding-cake of a building in this beau-tiful light.

She walked the short path past the side of the inn. The porch stretched around the sturdy, cream-painted exterior, the lines symmetrical, the green shingles on the gabled roof pristine. Green shutters framed the windows, ready to protect when storms came in.

For some reason, the main entrance didn't face the sand dunes and Lake Michigan, or even the parking lot on the other side. Instead, it faced north, looking down the hill like a mother hen.

Or a hunter.

She turned away from the inn, checked the distance, walked some more. Tried to frame the shot, walked back a little farther. She had to get the turret in, its forest-green gable roof vivid against the softening sky. That part of the inn had always been her favorite. Even besides it being Gran's private rooms, there was something magical about it. Like it had been plucked out of a fairy-tale and bolted directly onto the rest of the Queen Anne-style resort.

Just as she got it all in, with the soft orange of near-sunset edging everything gold, perfect shot, the front door opened.

No—it swung open.

On its own.

Just the wind. Old houses did that. Definitely the wind and not—

The foyer beckoned through the open door, warm

light spilling onto the porch like an invitation. No one appeared. Just that open door and the sense of being watched, evaluated, measured by something that had no eyes but saw everything.

Ella climbed the six shallow steps on legs that felt less steady than she'd like. The porch boards creaked a greeting—different notes under each foot, like a wooden piano only the inn knew how to play. She paused at the threshold, one hand on the doorframe.

"Hello?" Her voice cracked slightly. She cleared her throat, tried again with more authority. She was the owner now, she should act like it. "It's Ella Thompson?"

The question mark betrayed her uncertainty. How did you announce yourself to a building? How did you claim ownership of something that felt older and more permanent than any human claim?

The silence stretched, filled with the sounds of an old building breathing. Pipes ticking, wood settling, the whisper of air through unseen spaces. Then, from somewhere deep inside, came the unmistakable chime of crystal against crystal. Like champagne glasses toasting.

Ella stepped inside.

The foyer embraced her with the scent of lemon polish and old wood and yes, definitely lilacs. The chandelier—the one that had shattered in a storm twenty years ago, she remembered her grandmother's tearful phone call—hung perfect and whole, casting rainbow patterns across the walls.

And there, on its pedestal by the front desk, sat the giant sand globe.

Her feet carried her forward without permission. It was exactly as she remembered. No, that was impossible. She'd seen it broken, had mourned its loss with the fierce grief of a child. Yet here it stood, the golden sand perfectly still, the tiny lynx on its dune watching with glittering emerald eyes that seemed to track her movement.

"Impossible," she breathed.

She reached out, fingertips barely grazing the cool glass—

The sand exploded into motion. Not a gentle swirl but a sudden golden storm that made her jump back. The sand formed shapes as it danced—was that a face? Two figures embracing? The lynx, running?

"It never does that."

Ella spun toward the voice. A woman stood in the shadows by the dining room—silver hair in a precise bun, navy cardigan buttoned to the throat, expression caught between sternness and something that might have been wonder.

Mrs. Frankl? Ella dredged the name from summer memories.

The woman stepped into the light, and yes, it was

her—Sarah's right hand, the tea room guardian, the woman who'd snuck Ella extra cookies when her mother wasn't looking. Her gaze was on the globe. "All the years I've been here, it never does that for strangers."

"I'm not a stranger," Ella said automatically. "I'm—"

"Ah," Mrs. FranklFrankl interrupted, but her dark eyes had warmed, kindness crinkling at the corners. "You're late. The inn has been waiting. It doesn't like to wait."

A laugh bubbled up, unexpected and slightly hysterical. "The inn doesn't—"

Every light in the foyer flickered. The sand globe swirled faster. Deep in the walls came a sound like the building itself was drawing breath.

"Okaaaay," Ella said.

The lights steadied. The sand settled. Mrs. Frankl almost—almost—smiled.

"I'll make tea," she announced, turning toward what Ella remembered as the kitchen. "You'll want to take a look around, remind yourself of the layout, before the guests return."

Guests?

Of course, the inn would carry on, in the interim. People who stayed at places like this made reservations months in advance.

Ella wasn't ready for guests.

Alone in the foyer, she felt the weight of the building's attention. It pressed against her skin like humidity, filled her lungs like perfume, made her bones ache with something that might have been homesickness if she'd let herself name it.

Her phone buzzed. Chicago, must be. She declined the call without looking at the screen, but couldn't ignore the text that followed.

Call me. Henderson project needs your input ASAP. BTW, heard about a developer interested in northern MI properties. Could be perfect buyer for your situation.

"Right," she said to the listening walls. To no one. " Tour first. Existential crisis later."

The stairs beckoned, and she climbed them with one hand on the well-polished banister. The third step creaked—the same creak, the same note, as if seventeen years were nothing. As if she'd never left.

The second floor hallway stretched before her to the right, doors closed but somehow expectant. She tried the first knob—locked. The second—also locked. The third turned easily, revealing the Lighthouse Keeper's Room in perfect readiness. Brass fixtures gleamed. The bed was made with military precision. Fresh flowers—impossible October roses—filled a vase by the window.

Who's been maintaining this? And how could they afford October roses?

The room didn't answer, but through the window, she saw something that made her heart stutter. The lighthouse on the distant shore—decommissioned for fifty years, dead as old stone—flickered with light. Just once. Just for a moment.

A warning. A welcome. A promise that nothing at the Starlight Arbor Inn was quite what it seemed.

Back in the hallway, more doors yielded to her touch. Each room was perfect, pristine yet personal, as if decorated for specific guests who hadn't arrived yet. The Rose Suite smelled of June gardens. The Harbor Master's Room echoed with the shadow of an echo of boat whistles. The Blue Room—

The Blue Room was locked. Not just locked—sealed.

She knew that room. Had spent every summer there as a child, writing stories about brave girls and magic lynxes and boys made of sand hair who knew how to fix broken things.

The door's refusal felt personal. Like rejection. Like the inn knew she'd left and wasn't ready to forgive.

"Fine," she told it. "Keep your secrets. I have plenty of my own."

The door remained unmoved by her bravado.

By the time she reached the end of the second floor, the sun was setting properly, painting the hall in shades of amber and rose. She turned back, passed the stairs.

The turret room door stood at the end of the hall, the innkeeper's private suite. Grandma's rooms.

Now hers.

Time to open that box of memories.

But not from the second floor door.

She stepped down the slightly curving stairs back to the first floor and crossed the lobby's parquet floor. The door to the innkeeper's public rooms was on this floor.

This door opened at her touch. The place was exactly as Gran Sarah had left it. A teacup sat on the round table by one of the two reading chairs by the fireplace, lipstick marks on the rim in Sarah's signature coral shade.

The round room always felt surprisingly spacious despite its compact footprint, with warm honey-colored hardwood floors that creaked a gentle welcome underfoot. Light poured through tall west-facing windows, casting the inset sage greet loveseat and the rest of the space in golden afternoon hues.

Tucked into the northwest curve, a compact kitchenette fit so seamlessly into the turret's architecture it felt like an afterthought that became essential. Cream-colored cabinets with glass fronts display mismatched vintage teacups and Sarah's collection of ceramic canisters, while a small sink beneath a circular window offers glimpses of the dunes beyond.

Ella went to pick up the tea cup, meaning to bring it

to the kitchenette, but Sarah's massive roll-top deck drew her attention first. On the eastern side, with a view of the parking lot and the woods to the side of the property, the desk with its many cubbies and hidden drawers always held surprises. The leather chair in front of it carried a soft gray cardigan along its back. On the desktop's green blotter, three items waited in a precise line: a leather journal, a brass key on a star-shaped charm, and an envelope with Ella's name in Sarah's careful script.

Gran Sarah, always the planner.

Ella pulled out the chair and sat. The sweater hugged her with lilacs and cinnamon. Her hands shook as she opened the letter.

*My dearest Ella,

I'm so glad you've come home. Everyone has been waiting for you.

This place is more than wood and memory. You know that, deep down, no matter what your mother may have told you. I know you've spent these long years trying to forget, but it hasn't worked, has it, dear?*

Ella's throat tightened. How did Gran know? All those birthdays, all those Christmases, wanting to call but hearing Mom's voice: "That woman, with her dangerous nonsense."

So she didn't.

*The inn chooses its keepers carefully. It chose me. And now, my darling girl, it will choose you.

The journal will help you understand. The key opens what needs opening when the time is right. Trust the inn. Trust Mrs. Frankl. Trust your heart.

And remember that some things are worth waiting for.

All my love, Grandma

P.S. The coffee maker is temperamental. It only works for family. You'll do fine.*

The letter crumpled in her grip.

A door slammed somewhere. Voices drifted in—the guests returning. The Davidsons, Mrs. Frankl had said. Real people with real reservations in a real inn that she really had no idea how to run.

"I can't do this," she told the empty, cluttered room.

The lights flickered once.

She must have blinked weird.

From her purse, her phone buzzed again. Chicago. Her real life. Her sane, predictable, mystery-free life where sand globes didn't storm and lights didn't flicker and magic wasn't real.

She let it ring.

Ella found the Davidsons settled in the front parlor with tea and cookies that smelled like childhood. An older couple, holding hands, wedding rings worn thin with decades. They gazed out the wide picture windows at the lake and sand and sky, heads tilted toward each other. As Ella entered, they both turned.

"You must be Sarah's granddaughter," Mrs. Davidson said warmly. "You have her eyes."

"Her spirit, too," Mr. Davidson added, though how he could know that from half a second of acquaintance was beyond Ella. Unless the inn had told him. Which, given the day's events, seemed entirely possible.

"Thank you," Ella managed. "I hope your room is comfortable?"

"Perfect," they said in unison, and then laughed at themselves.

"We honeymooned here," Mrs. Davidson explained. "Forty years ago. Your grandmother gave us the same room. Said it would remind us why we fell in love."

"And?" Ella couldn't help asking.

They exchanged a look that contained decades. "It's working," Mr. Davidson said simply.

After they retired—back to their apparently marriage-saving room—Ella found Mrs. Frankl in the lobby, wrapped in a bright yellow raincoat, watching the sand globe swirl with lazy contentment.

"Just the one couple, tonight," Mrs. Frankl said. "Off season weekday, and Wednesdays are the worst. But day after tomorrow, the real test begins."

"What happens Friday?"

"You meet the staff. And they meet you." Her smile was knife-sharp with possibility. "Sarah always said the building might choose you, but the people decide if you stay."

After she left, Ella stood alone in the lobby of her inheritance, her legacy, her problem. The sand globe swirled gently, the lynx inside seeming to pace its miniature dunes with purpose. Outside, the wind whispered, impossible, undeniable.

Dream a little dream for me.

Chapter Two

Liam Carter had three rules about early morning calls: they'd better involve fire, flood, or death—and even then, they could probably wait until after coffee.

The phone ringing at 5:47 AM broke all three rules with the kind of determination that suggested the universe had opinions about his Thursday.

"What?" He'd given up on polite greetings after the second ring.

"The pipes at the inn." Mrs. Frankl's voice could have frosted windows in July. "You need to come."

Liam sat up, instantly awake. Nobody called about the Starlight Arbor at this hour. Not since—

"Which pipes?" He was already reaching for yesterday's jeans, phone tucked between ear and shoulder.

"The ones about to burst."

He caught his reflection in the dresser mirror—sandy hair sticking up at angles that defied physics, eyes still heavy with sleep, the stubble that Katie used to complain about but secretly loved. Ancient history, that. "Are they currently bursting?"

"Not yet."

"Then how do you—" He stopped. Twenty years of knowing Mrs. Frankl had taught him that questioning her certainties was like arguing with gravity. Pointless and likely to end with you flat on your face. "I'll be there in twenty."

"Fifteen would be better. The new owner arrived last night."

The words landed like cold water. Sarah's granddaughter. The one from Chicago who hadn't been back since—well, since before his time. The one who'd inherit everything and probably sell it to the highest bidder.

"Still there in twenty," he said, but grabbed a cleaner shirt.

The drive from his little cottage in the words to the inn took him through Green Arbor as it yawned toward morning. Harbor Street lay empty except for Tom Fitzgerald opening the bakery, bringing out his chalkboard sign, flour already dusting his apron. The first light was just threading through the trees, painting everything in shades of pearl and shadow. September had been mild so far, but morning still bit with teeth, reminding everyone that winter was coiled and waiting.

The lake stretched ahead of him, its surface the color of old pewter. No wind yet—the water lay still as held breath, reflecting the pale sky perfectly. Mornings like this, he understood why his grandfather had never left, why his father couldn't imagine living anywhere else, why even Katie's leaving hadn't been enough to drive him away.

At Main, he turned left. Another block, and the inn appeared through the morning mist like something from a dream—or a nightmare, depending on your relationship with Victorian architecture. Three stories of opinions and gingerbread trim, the turret pointing toward heaven like Sarah's last prayer. The grounds looked good, he noted automatically. The mums he'd planted last week had survived the deer, and the—

A light glowed in the kitchen window.

Not electric light. Something warmer, golden, like candle flame magnified. It flickered as he watched, and for just a moment he could swear he saw a shadow pass across it. Too tall for Mrs. Frankl. Too graceful for a stranger fumbling in an unfamiliar kitchen.

The inn's particular, boy. His grandfather's voice, twenty years gone but still clear as morning. *You listen, it'll tell you what it needs.*

"Just pipes," Liam muttered, parking in his usual

spot, on the other side of some old beater of a Focus that had snagged Sarah's spot. "Copper, iron, and water."

The front door stood open despite the morning chill. He paused on the threshold, caught by the scent that rushed out to greet him—lilacs and lemon polish and something else, something that hadn't been there in the month since Sarah's death.

The sand globe on its pedestal swirled gently, golden sand forming lazy spirals. He'd never seen it move without someone touching it first.

"She's in the kitchen." Mrs. Frankl materialized from the shadows by the stairs, making him wonder if she'd perfected teleportation. "Making coffee."

"The coffee maker works?"

Mrs. Frankl's expression suggested this question was both expected and concerning. "For now."

The kitchen was exactly as he'd feared.

She stood in a spreading puddle, Sarah's grey cardigan hanging loose on her smaller frame, holding what had recently been a coffee pot handle. The rest of the pot appeared to have distributed itself across the kitchen in an abstract art installation. Water flowed from the coffee maker's base—not violently, but insistently, like a spring that had suddenly decided the kitchen needed a water feature.

"That's not the pipes," he said, because stating the obvious felt safer than having her catch him staring.

She turned, and his chest did something complicated. Chestnut curls escaped from what had probably started as a bun. Color-flecked eyes flashed with the kind of frustrated humor that came from accepting the absurd. Coffee grounds dotted her freckled nose like war paint, and her city-girl silk blouse and slacks were soaked through.

Beautiful. The word came unbidden, unwanted. Beautiful in that fierce, disheveled way of someone refusing to be defeated by circumstance.

"Quite astute." Her voice held Chicago in its vowels but something else too. Sarah's warmth, maybe, buried under years of elsewhere. "Are you going to help or provide commentary?"

"Both. Move left."

"Why—"

The ceiling tile dropped exactly where she'd been standing, adding acoustic dampness to the morning's chaos. How he'd known it would fall, he couldn't say. The inn had its ways of telling you things, if you listened.

If you were foolish enough to listen.

She stared at the tile, then at him. "How did you—"

"Lucky guess. Hold this." He handed her a bucket from under the sink, then dove under the cabinet to find the shut-off valve. She moved with him, catching water, anticipating when he'd need space. Their strange dance felt practiced, as if they'd done this before.

Which was impossible. They'd never properly met. He'd been careful about that, maintaining the inn from a distance whenever he knew she might visit. Safer that way. For everyone.

The water stopped abruptly, leaving them both breathing hard in the sudden silence.

"Thank you." She pushed wet curls from her face, leaving a streak of coffee grounds across her cheek. It shouldn't have been endearing. "I'm Ella. Thompson."

"Liam Carter." He scooted aways from her and stood carefully, maintaining professional distance despite the urge to wipe that smudge away. "Mrs. Frankl mentioned you'd arrived."

"At 5:47 in the morning?"

"The inn keeps its own schedule." He studied the coffee maker's remains. The pattern made no sense—scattered but precise, like someone had choreographed the destruction. "When did this start?"

"About thirty seconds after I told it I needed coffee for the guests." She laughed, short and sharp. "Which sounds insane. I know it sounds insane. I've been telling myself that since the sand globe—" She stopped, color rising in her cheeks.

"Since the sand globe what?"

"Nothing. Just... moved. When I touched it."

The kitchen seemed to hold its breath. Even the dripping stopped.

"It never moves for strangers," he said carefully.

"So Mrs. Frankl mentioned." She tugged the cardigan tighter, and something in Liam's chest twisted. Sarah's cardigan on Sarah's granddaughter in Sarah's kitchen. The inn knew what it was doing. "She also mentioned something about the inn being particular. You seem familiar with its... particularities."

"I'm the son part of Carter & Son, Green Arbor's finest fixer-uppers. We've maintained the inn and much of the grounds for twelve years. You notice things." Like how the roses bloomed out of season when the inn was happy. Like how doors stuck when the wrong people tried to enter. Like how the sand globe had gone still as death the day Sarah died and hadn't moved since.

Until now.

"Twelve years," she repeated. "You must have known my grandmother well."

She spoke of you constantly. Worried about you. Loved you.

"She was a force of nature," he said instead. "This place was her life."

Something flickered across her face—grief, maybe, or guilt. "I know. I should have—" She stopped, straightened her shoulders. "I need to check on the guests. The Davidsons—"

"Are probably still sleeping. It's not even six-thirty." He gestured at her coffee-soaked state. "You might want to…"

"Right. Yes. I'll just…" She moved toward the door, then paused. "The pipes. Mrs. Frankl said they'd burst?"

"I'll check them. Basement's my next stop anyway."

"I could come with you. Learn the systems." She said it like someone used to taking charge, making plans. City efficiency overlaying small-town morning chaos.

"All wet like that? You'll short a fuse."

She looked down, seemed to realize she was still dripping. "Right. Okay. I'll change and—"

The lights flickered. Once, twice. The third time, they went out entirely.

In the near darkness—where had those thunder clouds outside come from?—Liam heard her sharp intake of breath. Felt rather than saw her step closer. Her hand found his arm, fingers gripping through his flannel shirt.

"Generator's in the basement," he said, trying to ignore how right her touch felt. "Probably just—"

Light bloomed through the inn. Not electric light—something softer, warmer. It seemed to emanate from the walls themselves, a golden glow that made everything look like it was lit by honey and starlight.

"What is that?" Her whisper brushed his neck.

"No idea." But that was a lie. He'd seen this once before, when he was seven and his grandfather had brought him to fix a broken shutter. The inn had glowed just like this, welcoming someone home.

The light faded gradually, electric fixtures taking over as if nothing had happened. But Ella's hand stayed on his arm, her pulse rapid under his fingers when he covered her grip with his own.

"Old wiring," he said. "Sometimes does strange things."

She pulled away, taking her vanilla-and-coffee scent with her. "Does it also explain how you knew that tile would fall?"

"Experience." The lie came easily. He'd had years of practice explaining away the inn's impossibilities. "You work on a building long enough, you learn its patterns."

"Its patterns." She tested the words like she was tasting them. "Right. And the sand globe moving— that's a pattern too?"

He turned to face her fully. In the restored light, she looked like she'd been through a battle—wet, coffee-stained, exhausted. But her eyes held something fierce, a determination that reminded him of Sarah facing down a wind squall.

"You want the truth?"

"Please."

"I have no idea why the inn does what it does. Sarah used to say it had its own mind, its own heart. That it knew things." He shrugged. "After twelve years, I've stopped trying to rationalize it."

She studied him for a long moment. "But you don't believe in... magic or whatever this is."

"I believe in what I can fix." He gestured at the destroyed coffee maker. "Speaking of which, you'll need a new one. Henderson's Hardware opens at eight, but since Henderson's my sister, she might make an exception for you."

"Or," Mrs. Frankl said from the doorway, making them both jump, "you could use the backup in the pantry. Third shelf, behind the peppermint tea."

"There's a backup coffee maker?" Ella sounded hopeful.

"Sarah believed in redundancy." Mrs. Frankl's sharp eyes moved between them, noting their proximity, the hand-shaped damp spot on Liam's sleeve. "The Davidsons are stirring. Perhaps you'd like to dress before greeting them?"

Ella fled with as much dignity as someone could manage in dripping silk. Liam found himself watching her go, the way Sarah's cardigan swayed with her movement, how she automatically stepped over the creaky board by the stairs.

"She looks like her," Mrs. Frankl said quietly.

"Not really. Different coloring, different—"

"I meant she looks like she belongs here." Mrs. Frankl moved into the kitchen, into the pantry, already reaching for the backup coffee maker. "Even if she doesn't know it yet."

"She's probably planning to sell." He could taste the bitterness in his tone.

"Plans change." Mrs. Frankl set the coffee maker, an old urn-style model that looked like it could support a regiment on the counter with practiced efficiency. "The inn has ways of changing them."

Liam thought about Ella's hand on his arm, the way she'd moved with him like dance partners who'd never rehearsed. "I should check those pipes."

"Yes," Mrs. Frankl agreed. "You should."

But he lingered in the doorway, watching her rinse the filters, measure coffee grounds. "Why did you really call me?"

She paused, not turning. "The pipes—"

"Won't burst. We both know that. They never do."

"The inn wanted you here." She dropped a scoop of coffee into the giant filter. "Who am I to argue?"

The basement was exactly as he'd expected—pipes in perfect condition, no sign of impending catastrophe. He went through the motions anyway, checking joints and pressure, tightening things that didn't need tightening. Above him, footsteps crossed the floor. Ella's, lighter than Sarah's but with the same purposeful rhythm.

His phone buzzed. A text from his sister: *Heard Sarah's girl is back. Stop by the store later. Mom brought pie.*

Pie meant gossip. Pie meant his mother had already planned their wedding and named their children. Pie meant trouble.

Another text, this from his dad: Harrison property needs you at 9. Don't get distracted by that inn.

Too late for that warning.

By the time he emerged from the basement, the kitchen smelled like coffee and cinnamon. Ella had changed into jeans and a sweater—still designer, but at least weather-appropriate. Her hair was pulled back in a clip that was fighting a losing battle with her curls.

"No burst pipes?" She handed him a mug without asking if he wanted one. The coffee was perfect—strong, black, exactly how he liked it.

"Not today."

"But Mrs. Frankl knew to call you anyway." She leaned against the counter, studying him over her own mug. "At exactly the right time."

"Lucky timing."

"Sure. Like the ceiling tile was lucky." She set her mug down. "Look, I appreciate the help, but I need to know—is this normal? Should I expect prophetic maintenance calls and coffee maker rebellions on a daily basis?"

He wanted to lie, to give her the comfortable fiction that the Starlight Arbor was just another old building with quirks. But something in her eyes—that mix of fear and fascination—stopped him.

"Define normal."

"Seriously?"

"The inn's... responsive. Sarah used to say it reacts to people's needs, their emotions. When it likes someone, it tries to help. When it doesn't..." He thought of the real estate developer who'd tried to buy the inn five years ago. The man's car wouldn't start, his phone died, and every room he tried to enter locked itself. "It can be unwelcoming."

"And the coffee maker explosion?"

"Testing you, maybe. Or—" He stopped. Or welcoming you home in its own chaotic way. But that seemed too much to say to someone who'd been back less than twelve hours.

"Or?"

"Or it just really wanted you to have better coffee." He drained his mug. "I should go. Other properties to check."

"Will you—" She paused, color rising in her cheeks. Apple cheeks, freckled nose. Soft eyes that made you want to tell her everything. "Will you be back? I mean, for regular maintenance?"

He should say no. Should recommend someone else, someone who didn't remember her at five years old, dancing in the garden while stars fell around her like snow. Someone who wouldn't notice how the morning light caught the gold flecks in her eyes.

"Mrs. Frankl has my number," he said instead.

"Right. Of course." She walked him to the door, professional distance restored. "Thank you. For the coffee maker and the ceiling tile and not thinking I'm crazy."

"I don't think you're crazy." He paused on the porch, looking back at her framed in the doorway. The inn seemed to glow behind her, content as a cat with cream. "But maybe don't tell the coffee maker what you need. Just make the coffee."

Her laugh followed him down the steps. "Noted. Any other appliances I should avoid conversing with?"

"The mixer's been known to hold grudges."

"Great. Vindictive kitchen appliances. That'll look great in the listing."

The word 'listing' killed his smile. Right. She must be here to sell, to turn Sarah's life work into a line item on a spreadsheet. He'd do well to remember that.

But driving away, watching her in the rearview mirror—looking out over the dunes, cardigan pulled tight, morning light making a halo of her impossible hair —he knew he'd be back.

The inn wanted him there. And despite his better judgment, despite twelve years of careful distance, despite knowing how this story would end...

So did he.

Chapter Three

Their main coffee maker worked perfectly at 5:30 AM, which should have been Ella's first warning that Friday had plans.

She stood in the pre-dawn kitchen, watching the ancient machine produce a stream of liquid gold without so much as a wheeze of protest. Yesterday, it had staged an aquatic rebellion that left her soaked and Liam Carter trying not to smile. But this morning? It purred like a cat who'd not only gotten the cream but had plans for the butter dish too.

"Thank you," she told it, then immediately felt ridiculous. Though given yesterday's events, maybe talking to appliances was just part of inn ownership now. Next she'd be asking the toaster's opinion on her business plan.

The kitchen held that particular quality of silence that came before dawn—not empty but expectant, like a theater just before curtain rise. Pale light filtered through the windows, painting everything in shades of pearl and possibility. Outside, fog crept up from the lake, sneaking across the dune and into the valley below, wrapping around the inn's foundation like a living thing.

She hadn't yet caught up on sleep, despite Sarah's amazingly comfortable mattress, but adrenaline and excellent coffee made up the difference. She'd spent Thursday exploring the inn, sunshine chasing shadows that seemed to dance with memory. Every room she'd entered had been perfect—not just clean but alive, as if they'd all been holding their breath for her return.

The Lighthouse Keeper's Room with its brass fixtures that gleamed without polish. Dune's Whisper where the wallpaper seemed to shift in her peripheral vision. The Rose Suite that had flooded with phantom scent the moment she'd touched the doorknob. Each space felt less like a hotel room and more like a personality waiting to be introduced.

Maybe today, she'd be brave enough to go into town.

Now, fortified with caffeine and wrapped in Sarah's cardigan that smelled increasingly of home, Ella spread her laptop and papers across the butcher block island. "Modern Breakfast Service: A Proposal for Starlight

Arbor Inn." She'd used her best corporate template, complete with market analysis and projected revenue increases.

Quinoa breakfast bowls. Avocado toast with microgreens. A kombucha station. Gluten-free options. Instagram-worthy presentations that would put the inn on every travel blogger's radar.

She pulled out her phone and snapped photos of yesterday's water damage—the warped floorboard, the discolored ceiling tile that had fallen. All evidence that would need to be disclosed in the listing. "Kitchen requires updates," she murmured, making notes. "Plumbing issues, possible electrical concerns." The words felt clinical, safe. Much easier than thinking about how the coffee maker had somehow seemed... hurt.

The mixer on the counter hummed—actually hummed. Had it always been that shade of mint green, or did it seem more vibrant in the growing light? The eggs in the sliding-window refrigerator had somehow arranged themselves in perfect rows, sorted by size like obedient soldiers. Even the radio on the shelf, dusty and neglected-looking yesterday, gleamed as if someone had polished it in the night.

Everything was cooperating. Everything was ready. Everything was suspiciously, perfectly prepared for her modernization plans.

She really should have known better.

The first attack came at exactly 6:00 AM. Not 5:59. Not 6:01. Three sets of steps in perfect unison that echoed through the quiet inn like a starter's pistol.

Ella smoothed her cardigan, lifted her chin, and turned toward the door to the lobby. Time to face her reckoning.

They entered the kitchen in age order and stood in formation like a photograph from another era. The morning fog still swirled around their feet. Agnes in front, steel-gray hair pinned in a bun that could double as a architectural support. Behind her, Beatrice, softer-looking but with eyes that caught the light like a crow spotting silver. Last came Cordelia, the baby at merely forty-five, round and smiling with the particular contentment of someone who knew exactly where all the bodies were buried and had helped dig some of the holes.

The morning air they brought in with them carried the scent of the lake and something else—anticipation, maybe, or the particular charge that came before storms.

"You're up early," Agnes said, making it sound like Ella had broken some fundamental law of the universe.

"I wanted to go over some ideas—"

"Ideas?" Beatrice tested the word like a sommelier finding cork taint.

"Now, girls, let's hear her out." Cordelia's voice was

honey poured over gravel, sweet with an edge that could cut.

But they weren't looking at Ella. All three stared past her at the coffee maker, which chose that moment to gurgle with unmistakable satisfaction.

"It's working," Agnes said flatly.

"For her," Beatrice added, as if this were evidence of a crime.

"Without threats or promises?" Cordelia finished, doubt in the gravel.

They exchanged a look that contained entire Victorian novels' worth of subtext, decades of shared experience, and what Ella was beginning to suspect was a phone tree that had been activated the moment her car had crossed the city limits.

"Please, come in." Ella stepped aside, clutching her proposals like armor. "I've prepared some thoughts about modernizing our breakfast service—"

The word 'modernizing' had an immediate effect. Agnes's spine straightened impossibly further. Beatrice's eyes narrowed to slits that would make a cat proud. Even Cordelia's smile flickered like a candle in wind.

The air in the kitchen's expectant silence became charged, electric.

They arranged themselves around the island like judges at a tribunal—if tribunals were staffed by women in sensible shoes who'd perfected the art of disappointment over decades of practice. The first shaft of real morning light shot through the windows, catching the dust motes between them, making them dance like tiny golden warnings.

Ella spread her printouts with the same confidence she'd used to pitch million-dollar office renovations. "I've been analyzing current hospitality trends. Younger travelers are looking for unique, health-conscious experiences they can share on social media. If we introduced quinoa breakfast bowls, avocado toast with microgreens, maybe a kombucha station—"

"Sarah Porter's apple butter," Agnes interrupted, "has won blue ribbons at the county fair for thirty-seven years straight."

"Her cinnamon rolls," Beatrice added, voice trembling with emotion, "have been written about in the *Detroit Free Press.* The recipe goes back four generations."

"And you want to replace it with store-bought?" Cordelia's horror was gentle but somehow worse for it.

"Well," Ella admitted, her confidence wavering like the fog outside, "initially, until I learn the recipes—"

"You sound just like those hotel chain people," Agnes said, each word carved from granite and polished with grief. "All buzzwords and no heart."

"The inn won't like being sold," Beatrice added, a sob in her voice.

The collective intake of breath created a small vacuum in the kitchen. Every appliance fell silent. The refrigerator stopped humming. The coffee maker ceased its contented burbling. Even the dust motes seemed to pause mid-dance.

And then the radio—the ancient, dusty radio that Beatrice would later swear hadn't worked since the Clinton administration—crackled to life.

"Stars shining bright above you..."

The Mamas and the Papas filled the kitchen, crystal clear despite the radio's age, the song seeming to come from the walls themselves. Everyone froze as Mama Cass crooned about dreams and longing and finding your way home.

"Sarah always said," Agnes whispered, her stern façade cracking like ice in spring, "that song played when the inn had opinions."

The radio's volume increased slightly, as if in agreement.

Ella felt the floor shifting beneath her, metaphorically speaking. Though given the inn's tendencies, literally wouldn't have surprised her. "It's just a radio malfunction. Old wiring—"

"Nothing in this inn malfunctions," Beatrice corrected, and now there were tears in her eyes. "Everything is perfect."

"Which is why," Cordelia added gently, reaching out

to pat Ella's hand, "we should perhaps discuss these... modern additions... more carefully."

The touch was warm, callused from decades of kneading dough and folding sheets and caring for this place. Ella found herself blinking hard against unexpected moisture in her own eyes.

"I just wanted to help," she said, hating how small her voice sounded. "To make it better, more profitable—"

"Oh, sweetheart." Cordelia squeezed her hand. "Better than what?"

Through the window, the fog began to lift, revealing the lake in its morning glory—silver and pearl and endless. A second beam of sunlight broke through, illuminating Sarah's photo on the wall. In it, she stood with three younger women, all of them covered in flour and laughing at something beyond the camera's view.

"Tell me," Ella said suddenly. "Tell me about the recipes. About her. About all of it."

The sisters exchanged another look, but this one was different. Warmer. Like watching the sun break through after a long storm.

"Well," Agnes said, unbending slightly, "it started with the apple trees. Sarah's mother planted them in 1962..."

As Agnes talked, Beatrice moved to the stove, her hands

finding their way without conscious thought. Cordelia opened cabinets, pulling out ingredients that shouldn't have been fresh but somehow were. The kitchen began to fill with the scent of warm dough, butter, sharp apple cider.

Ella found herself drawn into their dance, hesitant at first but gradually finding the rhythm. They taught her to fold butter into dough with a motion like blessing. Showed her how to judge the eggs' freshness by their weight in her palm. Explained that the apple butter's secret wasn't in the spices but in the stirring—clockwise for hope, counterclockwise for letting go, figure eights for love.

"Your grandmother," Beatrice said as they worked, "she understood that food is memory. Each recipe carries stories. You serve someone her cinnamon rolls, they're not just tasting breakfast. They're tasting every Christmas morning, every celebration, every moment of feeling safe and loved and home."

"But what about growth?" Ella asked, wrist aching from stirring the apple butter. "What about bringing in new guests, expanding—"

"The inn brings in who needs to be here," Agnes said firmly. "Always has. Our job is to be ready when they arrive."

As if in response, footsteps sounded overhead. The Davidsons, probably, drawn by the scent of baking.

Then more footsteps—had new guests arrived without her knowledge?

"Did someone—"

"The young doctor checked in late last night," Cordelia said casually. "Mrs. Frankl's nephew. And the photographer. They found their own rooms. The inn's good about that when it likes someone."

"Found their own rooms?" Ella's corporate mind reeled. "But the liability—"

All three sisters looked at her with identical expressions of patient pity.

"The inn," Agnes said slowly, as if explaining to a child, "takes care of its own. Always has. The question is—are you its own?"

Before Ella could answer, the kitchen door swung open. Mrs. Frankl stood there in her perfect navy cardigan, but this morning something was different. She was almost smiling.

"The dining room," she announced, "is full."

"Full?" Ella abandoned the apple butter. "But we only have two couples—"

"Word travels," Mrs. Frankl said simply. "When the inn wakes up, people notice. They come."

Ella rushed to the dining room and stopped short in the doorway. Every table was occupied. The Davidsons sat by the window, looking years younger than they had yesterday. A young man with tired doctor's eyes sat alone, but his exhaustion seemed to be lifting with each sip of coffee. A woman with a camera bag chatted with a couple Ella didn't recognize. Another couple looked like older versions of that cute Liam Henderson from yesterday.

"How—"

"Same way it always happens," Agnes said from behind her. "The inn calls, and hungry hearts answer."

But they weren't just hungry for food, Ella realized, watching the dining room transform into something from her childhood memories. These people were hungry for connection, for a place that remembered what hospitality meant before it became a corporate checklist.

"We can't serve all these people," Ella whispered, panic rising. "I don't even know how they knew we were open—"

"We've got this," Beatrice said, already tying an apron around Ella's waist. "You just need to trust."

What followed was a ballet of controlled chaos. The sisters moved through the kitchen and dining room with practiced grace, each knowing exactly where the others would be. Ella found herself swept into their current, carrying plates she hadn't seen prepared, pouring coffee that never seemed to run out, watching in amazement as the perfect food appeared exactly when needed.

The young doctor—Marcus, she learned—sat with

exhausted eyes brightening as he ate Agnes's scrambled eggs. "These taste like the ones my grandmother made," he said wonderingly. "But she never wrote down the recipe."

The photographer, Kelsey, nearly cried over her first bite of cinnamon roll. "It's like Christmas morning when I was seven. How is that possible?"

And through it all, the inn hummed with contentment. The sand globe in the lobby swirled in lazy, satisfied spirals. Sunlight streamed through windows that seemed cleaner than they'd been an hour ago. Even the notoriously creaky third step fell silent, as if not wanting to disturb the magic.

"Your fancy toast," Cordelia murmured as she passed, nodding toward the corner table.

Ella looked. Her single attempt at avocado toast sat abandoned on the sideboard, but at the corner table, a young couple shared what looked like... She moved closer. It was avocado toast, but transformed. The bread was Sarah's sourdough, the avocado mixed with herbs from the garden, local microgreens arranged like a tiny forest, eggs from the Hendersons' chickens nestled on top.

"How did you—"

"Wasn't us." Agnes appeared at her elbow, voice gruff but not unkind. "That was all you. You just had to learn the inn's language first."

Ella stared at the plate, then at the sisters, then at the full dining room of people who'd somehow known to come. "I don't understand."

"Your grandmother didn't either, at first." Beatrice's voice was gentle now. "Took her years to learn that the inn doesn't need managing. It needs partnering."

"Evolution, not erasure," Cordelia added, smiling at Ella's recognition of her own corporate-speak. "New ideas through old wisdom. That's how magic grows."

The morning rush gradually slowed, guests lingering over final cups of coffee, exchanging contact information, making plans to return. As the last visitor left—it was, indeed, the Hendersons, promising to bring Liam tomorrow—Ella sank onto a chair, exhausted but oddly exhilarated.

Her corporate mind automatically started calculating. Twelve tables, average check of $18, that's over $200 in breakfast revenue alone. Bump it up five dollars, figure out how to flip four of the tables... this could offset the thin occupancy during midweek... She shook her head. There she was again, reducing magic to spreadsheets.

"That was..." She searched for words.

"A typical Friday when Sarah was alive," Agnes finished. "The inn's been sleeping since she passed. Waiting."

"For what?"

The three sisters looked at her with expressions that suggested the answer should be obvious.

"For you to come home," Mrs. Frankl said from the doorway. She held a cup of tea that smelled like sunshine and possibilities. "For you to stop trying to be what you think you should be and remember who you are."

"I'm a commercial properties manager from Chicago," Ella said automatically.

"No." Agnes's voice was firm but kind. "You're Ella Thompson, heir to a legacy of love and burned toast and magic apple butter. The girl who spent summers naming chipmunks and building fairy houses in the garden."

"The girl who danced with that Carter boy under stars," Beatrice added with a sly smile.

"The girl who belongs here," Cordelia finished, "whether she's ready to admit it or not."

Ella looked around the kitchen—at the perfectly behaved coffee maker, the mixer that had stopped humming and started purring, the radio that played soft jazz as if it had never thrown its morning tantrum. Through the window, she could see the lake sparkling in full morning sun, and was that Liam's truck pulling into the drive?

"What if," she said slowly, "we kept the traditional menu but added a few modern options? Locally sourced, seasonally inspired. Evolution, not erasure, like you said."

The sisters exchanged one of their telepathic looks.

"Now," Agnes said, the ghost of a smile creaking across her face, "you're talking."

"But first," Beatrice added, eyes twinkling as Liam's truck door slammed, "you might want to fix your hair. You've got apple butter, there." She pointed to a spot above Ella's left ear.

Ella's hand flew to her head, finding the sticky streak just as footsteps sounded on the porch. The sisters scattered like teenagers caught plotting, leaving her alone with her apple-butter hair and racing heart as Liam Cunningham appeared in the doorway.

"Heard you had quite the breakfast rush," he said, and was that warmth in his voice? "Thought I'd check if anything needed fixing."

Yes, Ella thought, pulse jumping as his blue eyes found hers. My entire understanding of how the world works. My five-year plan. My ability to think straight when you look at me like that.

"Just the usual," she said instead. "Prophetic appliances, magical recipes, impossible guests appearing from nowhere. You know, normal inn stuff."

His smile was slow and devastating. "So you're starting to speak its language."

"Apparently I'm bilingual. Corporate buzzword and

magical inn." She gestured helplessly at the kitchen, still warm with the ghost of the morning's chaos. "Who knew?"

"Sarah knew." He stepped inside, bringing the scent of sawdust and morning air. "She always said you'd come back when you were ready to hear it."

Something twisted in Ella's chest—grief and guilt and something else, something that felt dangerously like hope. "Did she talk about me a lot?"

"Only every day." His voice gentled. "Especially near the end. She'd sit on the porch, watching for your car, even though..." He stopped, but the words hung between them. Even though you never came.

"I should have—"

"You're here now." He moved closer, and she could see gold flecks in his blue eyes, could count the laugh lines that suggested he smiled more than his serious expression let on. "That's what matters."

The kitchen held its breath. Even the appliances seemed to lean in.

"Liam," she started, not sure what she was going to say. That she was scared? That she was planning to sell? That the way he looked at her made her reconsider everything?

But footsteps thundered down the stairs, breaking the moment. Marcus Chen appeared in the doorway, looking marginally less exhausted but significantly more puzzled.

"Sorry to interrupt," he said, though his eyes suggested he knew exactly what he'd interrupted. "But my room—the lighthouse room?—the actual lighthouse outside my window just turned on. In broad daylight. Is that... normal?"

Ella and Liam exchanged glances.

"Define normal," they said in unison, then looked at each other in surprise.

Marcus's laugh was rusty but genuine. "Right. Magic inn. Sure. I'm just going to... go with it." He grabbed a muffin from the counter—one that definitely hadn't been there a moment ago—and headed back upstairs. "Oh, and there's a photographer lady stuck in the Blue Room. Door won't open. She seems pretty calm about it, though. Says the light is perfect for portraits."

After he left, Ella buried her face in her hands. "I run a magic inn. I live in a magic inn that locks photographers in rooms and turns on lighthouses and makes impossible muffins appear."

"You forgot the part where it plays matchmaker," Liam said quietly.

She peeked at him through her fingers. "What?"

"The lighthouse only turns on when—" He stopped, color rising in his cheeks. "Never mind. I should check on that door. The Blue Room gets ideas sometimes."

"More opinions? Great. Because the coffee maker wasn't judgmental enough."

His laugh followed him up the stairs, warm and rich and making her want to follow just to hear it again.

Ella stood alone in the kitchen, surrounded by the evidence of the morning's magic—empty plates that had held impossible food, flowers that had definitely not been in that vase an hour ago, and a sense of belonging she hadn't felt in seventeen years.

Her phone chirped. Another email from Chicago, another crisis that felt suddenly unimportant.

Subject: Time-Sensitive: Q4 Planning

Ella,

Your "quick assessment" is taking considerably longer than discussed. I've attached the posting for Senior Director of Acquisitions. Application deadline is October15. I don't need to tell you that remote candidates won't be considered.

Also, Pinnacle Hospitality Group called about your assessment. They're VERY interested in underdeveloped lakefront properties. This could be your ticket to the next level.

Call me.

MS

She couldn't think about that now. She pocketed the phone to find Agnes standing in the doorway.

"So," the older woman said, approval creaking into her voice, "same time tomorrow?"

"I... yes. If you'll have me. Teach me."

Agnes's nod was queenly. "Five-thirty sharp. The inn doesn't respect lazy mornings." She paused at the door. "And Ella? Wear something you don't mind getting flour on. The mixer's been patient so far, but it's got seventeen years of mischief stored up."

After she left, Ella walked into the lobby. The sand globe was sleeping. Upstairs, she could hear Liam's voice mixing with Kelsey's laughter. Must've unjammed the door.

The inn hummed around her, alive and magical and terrifying and home.

Her phone buzzed again. This time she turned it off entirely.

Chapter Four

Liam had left the inn Friday afternoon with Kelsey's grateful thanks and the Blue Room door working perfectly, though he was fairly certain it had never actually been stuck. He'd driven home telling himself he'd done his job, that he could stay away for a few days, let the new innkeeper settle in without him hovering like a lovesick teenager or something.

That resolution had lasted exactly eighteen hours.

Now, Saturday mid-morning, he had three perfectly logical reasons for returning: to check the Stargazer Suite door that sometimes wouldn't open, the occasionally loose floorboard on the second-floor landing, and the kitchen faucet that had developed an intermittent drip.

None of them explained why he'd showered twice or why his toolbox contained items he definitely hadn't put there—like the small bottle of WD-40 that smelled inexplicably of lilacs.

The morning was crisp with autumn's promise, lake fog already burnt off and the dunes shimmering golden in the distance. He parked beside Ella's battered Focus, which sat slightly askew in Sarah's old spot, as if it too was still figuring out where it belonged. The scent of woodsmoke drifted from someone's chimney, mixing with the ever-present smell of lake water and the last wild roses clinging to the inn's front trellis.

The inn rose before him against the clear blue sky, every window catching light like crystal. For just a moment, watching the way the turret reached toward the sky, he could almost hear his grandfather's voice: *This place has been waiting for something. Can you see it?*

Twenty-three years later, Liam was beginning to suspect he knew what.

The front door stood open—typical for morning checkout time, though he could hear the gentle clatter of breakfast dishes and the murmur of voices from the dining room. The familiar scents of the inn wrapped around him as he stepped inside: wood polish, fresh coffee, and vanilla.

Mrs. Frankl materialized from the shadows like she'd

been expecting him, her sensible shoes silent on the polished floors.

"Third floor," she said without preamble, her voice carrying its usual crisp efficiency. "The Stargazer Suite door won't open. Mrs. Henderson is quite frustrated."

"Stuck?" Liam shifted his toolbox, feeling the weight of tools he'd somehow gathered without conscious thought.

"Completely. She's just called down from the phone in the library." Mrs. Frankl's expression was carefully neutral, but something flickered in her eyes. "Though I suppose it doesn't matter much longer."

"What do you mean?"

"Sarah's granddaughter. Probably already has a buyer lined up." Her voice carried that particular tone reserved for discussing necessary evils. "Corporate types don't usually keep sentimental guests."

Before he could respond, she was already gliding away toward the kitchen, leaving him with the lingering scent of her lavender soap and a knot of unease in his stomach.

The stairs creaked their familiar greeting as he climbed, each step steady solid wood after decades of careful maintenance. His grandfather's hands had touched this banister, his boots had worn smooth places in these treads. The weight of that history pressed against Liam's chest as he climbed.

The second floor hallway was empty, doors closed but somehow expectant. As he passed the Lighthouse Keeper's Room, he could hear Dr. Chen moving around inside—the soft thud of a book being set down, the rustle of papers. From the Dune Walker's Room came the muffled crash of a backpack hitting the floor, followed by a woman's muttered "Perfect."

The photographer. Kelsey something. She'd arrived Thursday night, according to the town gossip network, though nobody seemed to know exactly when she'd made the reservation.

The third floor felt different as he reached it—charged, like the air before a storm. The scent was different too, sharper somehow, with an undercurrent of ozone that made the hair on his arms stand up. And there, at the near end of the hall, stood Mrs. Henderson.

Janet Henderson, seventy-three, her steel-gray hair that never had a strand out of place and the posture of someone who'd spent forty years teaching high school English. Right now, though, she looked thoroughly flustered, her usually immaculate appearance slightly disheveled as she stood before the Stargazer Suite door with her hands planted firmly on her hips.

"Oh, thank goodness," she said when she spotted him, relief flooding her voice. "This door is being absolutely impossible. I've stayed in this room dozens of times, and it's never—" She rattled the antique brass doorknob with the kind of frustrated vigor that suggested she'd been at this for a while.

"Let me take a look." He set his toolbox down on the midnight-blue carpet, the metallic clink of tools unnaturally loud in the charged air. The doorknob was warm under his fingers—warmer than it should be, given the cool morning. The brass seemed to pulse slightly, like a heartbeat just barely perceptible through metal.

"It's the strangest thing," Mrs. Henderson continued, her usual composure cracking slightly around the edges. "Harold and I have been coming here for forty-seven years. Well, forty-five years now, since he..." Her voice caught, and she cleared her throat with determined dignity. "This has always been our room. The Stargazer Suite. Harold proposed to me in this room, you know, right by that curved window overlooking the lake."

Liam tested the lock mechanism, feeling the familiar resistance of old hardware. But there was something else —a sense that the door wasn't stuck so much as... waiting. "Forty-seven years," he said, buying time while he worked. "That's a lot of history."

"Sarah was just a young thing when we first started coming. Younger than that granddaughter of hers." Mrs. Henderson's voice carried a wistful note. "She used to say this room had opinions about who belonged in it. I always thought she was being fanciful, but..." She gestured helplessly at the unyielding door.

The lock mechanism suddenly gave way under his fingers with a soft click that seemed to echo longer than it should. The door swung open with the satisfied sigh of well-oiled hinges, releasing a rush of air that carried the impossible scent of aftershave. Old Spice?

Mrs. Henderson stepped across the threshold first, and Liam saw her spine straighten as she breathed in. "Oh," she whispered, her voice thick with memory. "That scent..."

She moved toward the center of the room, and Liam followed, his boots silent on the thick midnight blue carpet. The Stargazer Suite was exactly as he remembered from his childhood visits with his grandfather—circular walls following the curve of the turret, windows that wrapped around the space like an embrace, the hand-painted constellation ceiling that had fascinated him as a boy.

"Harold always said this room felt like sleeping inside a star," Mrs. Henderson was saying, her voice growing stronger as she moved to touch the curved window frame. Even the cushions of the inset window seats were that midnight blue. "He'd stand right here and point out the real constellations, match them to the ones painted overhead. Said it was like—"

She stopped mid-sentence, her body going rigid.

Liam followed her gaze to the dark-oak circular nightstand beside the bed. Something on the nightstand caught the morning light streaming through the windows.

A ring. Simple gold band, well-polished, sitting precisely in the center of the wooden surface as if someone had just carefully placed it there.

The air in the room went absolutely still. Even the ever-present lake breeze seemed to pause, waiting.

"That's..." Mrs. Henderson's voice was barely a whisper. "Impossible."

Liam felt the bottom drop out of his world. He'd been looking at that nightstand when they entered—had seen it clearly, the wood grain, the small lamp, the way the light shone across the empty surface.

The ring hadn't been there thirty seconds ago.

Now it sat there like it had been there all night, warm with the glow of well-loved gold.

Mrs. Henderson took a step toward the nightstand, then another, moving like someone afraid the mirage might vanish. Her hand reached out, trembling, and touched the ring with one fingertip.

"It's real," she breathed. "It's really..."

Her knees buckled.

Liam moved without thinking, catching her elbow as she swayed, guiding her backward to the cushioned window seat. She collapsed onto it with a soft sound that was half laugh, half sob. She took in a shaky breath.

"I lost this ring three years ago," she whispered, staring at the band still sitting on the nightstand. "In Chicago, of all places. Harold and I were visiting our daughter, and I took it off to wash dishes. It went down the drain, and the plumber said..."

She shook her head, a few strands of hair escaping from its careful arrangement. "Gone. Harold died a month later, and I thought I'd lost the last piece of him I could touch."

The air in the room hummed—actually hummed—with something that definitely wasn't the heating system. The constellation ceiling seemed to pulse gently.

Liam's mouth was dry as dust. His hands shook slightly as he knelt beside Mrs. Henderson's seat. "Mrs. Henderson..."

"You saw it too," she said, looking up at him with eyes bright with tears and wonder. "You saw it appear. I'm not going crazy, am I? You saw it happen."

He had seen it. Had watched that ring materialize on the nightstand. Had felt the air change.

"I saw it," he said quietly.

Mrs. Henderson's laugh was pure joy, bright and startling in the charged air. She stood carefully and moved to the nightstand, lifting the ring with reverent fingers. It slipped onto her finger like it had never been gone. The moment it settled into place, the room filled with warmth—not heat, but the kind of warmth that came from being exactly where you belonged.

"Harold," she whispered to the empty air. "You impossible, wonderful man."

The scent of aftershave grew stronger for just a moment, and then faded, leaving only the clean smell of lake air and the lingering warmth of love that refused to be lost.

Liam's grandfather's voice echoed in his memory: *The inn doesn't just shelter bodies, child. It shelters hearts.*

And sometimes hearts need what they think they've lost forever.

Footsteps on the stairs interrupted the reverent quiet, quick and light. Ella appeared in the doorway, hair a cloud escaping from her loose ponytail, flour dusting her left shoulder. She took in the scene—Mrs. Henderson's tear-streaked face, Liam kneeling by the window seat probably looking like he'd seen a ghost.

"Is everything okay? I heard—" Her gaze fell on the ring, and her face went pale. "Oh. Oh no."

"Oh no?" Mrs. Henderson's voice sharpened with protective instinct. "What do you mean, oh no?"

Ella shot Liam a look that was pure panic.

"You're engaged?"

Liam shot to his feet.

"It's just that... the ring." Ella closed her eyes a

moment, visibly calming herself. She opened them again, her face struggling to show serenity. "That's such a beautiful ring."

"It's not mine," Liam said, not sounding guilty at all. "It came from Chicago."

"It's mine," Mrs. Cunningham saved him. "And Harold's."

"Oh!" Relief flooded Ella's face. "You found it!"

"It found me." Mrs. Henderson held her hand up, admiring the ring. "It was waiting for me, on the nightstand."

Ella's smile froze. Her gaze snapped to Liam, the beginnings of panic at the edges of her eyes. "That's... unexpected."

"Unexpected," Mrs. Henderson repeated slowly, her teacher's instincts clearly detecting evasion. "If I didn't know better, I'd say this inn was haunted."

"Haunted? No! Absolutely not." Ella's voice climbed an octave. The sharp scent of adrenaline mixed with her vanilla-and-flour sweetness. "That would be... haunted means ghosts, and we don't have ghosts. We have character. Personality. Sometimes the, um, personality gets a little—"

A door slammed somewhere below them. Then another. Then what sounded like several doors slamming in rapid succession, like dominoes falling through the inn's three floors.

Mrs. Henderson raised an eyebrow. "Personality?"

"Enthusiastic personality," Ella amended weakly, her cheeks flushing pink.

They heard footsteps running up the stairs, followed by voices—a young man's concerned baritone mixing with a woman's laughter that sounded surprisingly delighted rather than alarmed.

Dr. Chen—Marcus—appeared first, slightly out of breath, dark hair mussed like he'd been napping. The scent of coffee and soap clung to him. Behind him came the photographer—Kelsey, wide awake her camera in hand, dressed for hiking in clothes. Her eyes were bright with curiosity.

"Did anyone else's door just—" Marcus started.

"Open itself? Yes." Kelsey grinned. "I was in the hall, coming back from breakfast. The lighthouse room's door opened, and my dune room's door opened. I swear I saw them open in sequence like some kind of..." She paused, studying the assembled group with the sharp attention of someone used to capturing perfect moments. "Like the inn was introducing us."

For a moment, Marcus and Kelsey looked at each other, really looked. His eyes were kind behind wire-rimmed glasses, the sort of steady calm that came from making life-and-death decisions in emergency rooms. She had the restless energy of someone always chasing the next perfect shot, but her gaze lingered on his face like she might've found something worth staying still for.

The air between them practically sparked.

"So," Kelsey said, not looking away from Marcus, "anyone else getting the feeling this place has opinions about who should meet whom?"

Mrs. Henderson laughed, sudden and delighted, the sound bright as silver bells. "Oh my dear, that's exactly what this place does. Harold and I met here forty-seven years ago when a storm knocked out the power and we huddled in the library by the fire. Same fire, one blanket." She held up her ring, letting it catch the light streaming through the curved windows. "Some things are meant to be found again."

Ella made a small, strangled sound. Liam found himself moving closer to her, ostensibly to retrieve his toolbox from the hallway but really because she looked like she might faint.

"Mrs. Henderson," Ella tried again, her voice carefully controlled, "about the ring—"

"It's a miracle," the older woman said firmly, her teacher's voice brooking no argument. "Whether it's magic or coincidence or Harold reaching across whatever comes after, I don't care. I have it back." She looked around the room, taking in the constellation ceiling, the curved windows full of blue-white midday light, the way the space seemed to pulse with gentle warmth. "This place has always been special."

Mrs. Henderson moved toward the door, pausing to pat Ella's hand with fingers that were warm and sure. "Thank you, dear. For keeping the magic alive."

After she left, the four of them stood in awkward silence. The room still hummed faintly, like a tuning fork slowly settling back to silence. Marcus cleared his throat first, the sound unnaturally loud.

"I'm Marcus," he said, extending his hand to Kelsey. "Mei-Li—Mrs. Frankl—is my auntie. She told me I had to come. Said I needed a rest. But I'm beginning to think this weekend is going to be more interesting than I planned."

"Kelsey." Her handshake lingered a moment longer than strictly necessary. "Dune Walker's Room. And you're in the Lighthouse Room, right? I heard you mention the lighthouse turning on."

"Good guess."

"Mind if I photograph your reaction when the lighthouse turns on again tonight? Because I have a feeling it's going to."

They left together, Marcus's steady voice mixing with Kelsey's animated chatter as they descended the stairs, their footsteps creating a rhythm that sounded almost like music. Which left Liam alone with Ella in a room that still hummed with impossible possibilities.

The scent of Old Spice had faded, but something warmer remained—the smell of happiness, if happiness had a smell. Like bread baking and flowers blooming and all the small joys that made a house a home.

Ella immediately turned to Liam, panic bright in her eyes. "Please," she said, gripping his arm. She had a good grip. "You can't tell anyone about this. I can't have people thinking the inn is haunted. How would I even put that in a property report? 'Guest room occasionally manifests long-lost jewelry'?"

"Property report?" His voice was carefully neutral, but his chest tightened at the words.

She was still thinking of selling. Of course she was.

"I just... people will think I'm running some kind of tourist trap. Or worse, they'll want proof, documentation..." She sank onto the window seat where Mrs. Henderson had just been, head in her hands. A shaft of sunlight caught the gold threads in her brown hair. "This is a disaster. She's going to tell everyone the inn is haunted. Word will spread. Ghost hunters will come. Or worse, paranormal investigators with terrible TV shows."

"Or," Liam said carefully, settling beside her on the window seat, "she'll tell everyone the inn is magical. And people who need magic will come."

Ella looked up at him through her fingers, and he could see the fear and wonder warring in her expression.

"You saw it too, right? You looked like you'd seen a ghost." She looked around the room, as if sweeping it for landmines with her gaze. "That ring. There's no logical explanation for how it got here."

He could give her one. Could talk about how old buildings settled, how small objects could fall into cracks and work their way back out over years. Could mention that Mrs. Henderson was seventy-three and grief did strange things to memory and perception.

But he'd seen the ring appear. Had watched it materialize on that nightstand like someone invisible had just set it down with infinite care. Had felt the air change, charged with love that refused to be lost.

"No logical explanation," he agreed.

"So what do I do? How do I run a business when the business defies physics?"

Liam let himself really look at her—the flour in her hair, the way her hands shook slightly when she was nervous, the small scar on her chin that suggested a childhood filled with adventure. This close, he could smell her uncertainty, sharp and metallic, but underneath it was something warmer.

"You could embrace it," he said quietly.

"Embrace haunted inn status?"

"Embrace what it actually is." He gestured at the room around them, the way the light seemed to dance across the curved cream walls in patterns that suggested more than mere refraction. The constellation ceiling pulsed gently overhead, and he could swear he felt the inn listening. "Sarah never advertised the inn as magical, but people knew. Word spread anyway. They came because they needed what this place offers."

"Which is?"

"Hope. Second chances. The possibility that impossible things happen when you need them most." He thought of Mrs. Henderson's face when she'd seen that ring, the wonder and joy and healing in her tears. The scent of happiness that still lingered in the air. "Some people call that magic. Others call it love. Maybe they're the same thing."

Ella was quiet for a long moment, studying his face with an intensity that made his skin warm. Her eyes were the color of autumn leaves, brown and gold and green all mixed together.

"You believe it? That it's magic?"

It wasn't quite a question, but he answered anyway, tasting the truth of it on his tongue like copper and honey. "I used to. When I was little, my grandfather would bring me here to help with repairs. He'd tell me stories about the inn, about the things he'd seen." Liam's voice went soft with memory. "Rooms that matched themselves to guests' needs. Objects that appeared exactly when someone needed them. Couples who met in impossible ways and just... knew."

"What changed?"

"I grew up. Started explaining things away. Told myself it was coincidence, confirmation bias, the power of suggestion." He looked down at his hands, hard from years of fixing things that could be fixed, tools that followed logical rules and mechanical principles. "Easier than believing in something you can't control or understand."

"And now?"

"Now I've watched a lost wedding ring appear from three hundred miles away to comfort a grieving woman. And I've seen you walk into this place and watch it come alive again." He met her eyes, saw his own uncertainty reflected there, but something else too—possibility, bright and warm as summer sunshine. "I'm running out of explanations that don't involve magic."

The air between them seemed charged, like the moment before lightning strikes. Ella's hand rested on the window seat between them, small and freckled and somehow perfect. Without thinking, he covered it with his own.

The reaction was immediate. The constellation ceiling pulsed once, as if some cosmic heartbeat had skipped. The scent of lilacs filled the air—not the lilacs from his mysterious WD-40, but deeper, richer, like the ghost of a perfume worn by someone who'd loved this place with her whole heart.

Ella stared at their joined hands, her pulse a butterfly, her skin warm and soft. "That's not normal."

"No," he agreed, but he didn't pull away. Her hand fit perfectly under his, like two pieces of a puzzle finally finding their place. "But maybe normal is overrated."

"Liam..." Her voice was breathless, uncertain, and he could taste her fear in the air—sweet and sharp like green apples.

"I know." He lifted their joined hands, studying the way her smaller fingers fit between his, the contrast of her pale skin against his weathered tan. "I know this is crazy. I know you're probably going to sell this place and go back to Chicago and forget all about small-town handymen who believe in magic."

"I'm not—" She stopped, color rising in her cheeks like sunrise. "I don't know what I'm going to do."

"That's okay." He squeezed her hand gently, feeling her pulse steady under his thumb. "The inn's patient. It waited seventeen years for you to come back. It can wait a little longer for you to decide if you want to stay."

From downstairs, Mrs. Frankl's voice rang out, greeting new arrivals. The inn's business continued— footsteps on stairs, doors opening and closing, the distant murmur of voices in the drawing room.

Liam released Ella's hand, immediately missing the warmth of her skin against his. His fingers tingled where they'd touched hers. "I should check that door," he said, though his voice came out rougher than intended. "Make sure it's working properly now."

"Right. The door." She stood, smoothing her hair with hands that shook slightly. "Professional maintenance. Very important."

He tested the door mechanism, found it working perfectly. The brass knob was cool now, normal temperature, normal feel. Of course it was. The inn had gotten what it wanted.

"Seems to be fine now," he said, though they both knew the door had never been broken.

"Of course it is." Ella's smile was rueful, but there was something else there too—acceptance, maybe, or the beginning of it. "Thank you. For coming. For... understanding."

"Anytime." He hefted his toolbox, the tools inside settling with their familiar metallic whisper. As he crossed the threshold, he paused. "And Ella? Mrs. Henderson won't cause trouble. People who find what they've lost here tend to become the inn's biggest protectors."

"How do you know?"

"Because that's what it does. The inn doesn't just give people what they've lost. It gives them reasons to make sure no one else loses what they've found."

He left her standing in the turret room, sunlight painting her in shades of gold and possibility. As he descended the stairs, he could hear Marcus and Kelsey's animated voices drifting from somewhere outside—something about hiking trails and lighthouse schedules and the way morning light looked different through curved windows.

In the lobby, Mrs. Frankl stood by the sand globe, which was swirling in lazy, contented spirals. The golden sand caught the light from the tall windows, creating patterns that looked almost like stars, almost like a map of somewhere wonderful.

"Door fixed?" she asked without looking up, her voice carefully neutral.

"Door was never broken."

"Mmm." She didn't sound surprised. "And Mrs. Henderson?"

"Found what she was looking for."

Mrs. Frankl's smile was small but satisfied.

Nothing else needed fixing. The loose floorboard had somehow tightened itself, and when he checked the kitchen faucet, it ran smooth and silent. But whatever that electrical thing was going on between him and the new innkeeper—that definitely needed... something.

As Liam drove away, he found himself thinking about wedding rings that traveled across states to find their way home. About doors that opened at precisely the right moments. About the way Ella's hand had felt in his, small and warm and perfectly right.

By the time he reached his cottage, he'd stopped trying to explain any of it away.

Some things, his grandfather had always said, couldn't be understood. They were meant to be believed.

Guess it was time to start believing again.

Chapter Five

Ella had been staring at her laptop screen for twenty minutes, cursor blinking accusingly in the Google search bar. She'd typed and deleted a dozen variations: "How to run a haunted hotel," "Wedding rings appearing out of nowhere," "Is my inherited inn possessed," and her personal favorite, "How to explain magic to insurance companies."

None of them seemed likely to yield practical business advice.

The afternoon sun danced through the main floor turret room windows, warming the small sitting area where she'd set up her temporary office. Sarah's roll-top desk felt too personal, too much like trespassing, so she'd claimed the window seat with its sturdy sage cushions, hefty cream pillows, and its view of the lake and the old lighthouse that had absolutely, definitely not flickered on and off last night.

The memory of Mrs. Henderson's wedding ring still made her chest tight. Liam's face, so pale. Mrs. Henderson, glowing with the sun behind her.

Nothing explained it.

Her phone buzzed. The name "Markie Sohn" flashed on the screen with a photo of her boss—sharp suit, sharper smile, the woman who'd taught her that every property was just numbers on a spreadsheet if you looked at it the right way.

How's the property assessment going? You promised those numbers by Monday.

Monday. Right. The real world, where properties were assets and magic wasn't a line item in quarterly reports.

She was still contemplating whether "miraculous object manifestation" qualified as a unique selling point when a knock sounded on the door to the lobby. Mrs. Frankl appeared, carrying a tray that held an ornate silver tea service and wearing an expression that suggested Ella's afternoon was about to become significantly more complicated.

"Time for your education," Mrs. Frankl announced. She swept the hurricane lamp off the round table in the sitting area and set the silver platter on it instead. She set the lamp on the driftwood shelf over the fireplace, which had been built of local stones worn smooth by sand and surf.

"Education in what?"

"Tea service. If you're going to run this inn, you need to understand all its operations." Mrs. Frankl's dark eyes held the particular gleam of someone who'd been planning this moment since Ella's arrival. "The tea room isn't just another amenity. It's the heart of what we do here."

Ella closed her laptop with a soft click. "I thought the heart was the guest rooms. Or the dining service. Or possibly the magical sand globe that predicts romantic outcomes."

"The tea room," Mrs. Frankl repeated firmly, ignoring the sarcasm entirely, "is where healing happens. Where people remember who they were before life wore them down to shadows."

She began arranging items from the tray with the focus of a surgeon preparing for operation. Each piece—teapot, cups, saucers, a collection of small ceramic containers—found its designated place as if choreographed.

Ella drifted over to the sitting area, cautiously interested. She passed over the worn leather reading chair in favor of the one in faded floral fabric. It seemed more appropriate.

"Sarah started the formal tea service in 1987," Mrs.

Frankl continued, her voice softening with memory. "Said people needed ritual, ceremony, a reason to slow down and remember that some things couldn't be rushed."

"Like what?"

"Like grief. Like healing. Like learning to love again after you've convinced yourself you're broken." Mrs. Frankl lifted one of the ceramic containers, removing the lid to reveal loose tea leaves that smelled of jasmine. "Each blend serves a purpose. This one's for new beginnings."

Ella found herself leaning forward despite her skepticism. "You choose the tea based on what people need?"

"The tea chooses itself, mostly. You just have to listen." Mrs. Frankl measured leaves with an antique silver spoon, movements economical and sure. "Your grandmother had the gift. Could look at someone and know exactly what blend would help them find their way."

"And you think I—"

"I think you've been asking the wrong questions." Mrs. Frankl poured steaming water from a kettle that definitely hadn't been steaming a moment ago. "Instead of asking if you can run this place, ask if you're willing to let it run through you."

The words hung in the air like incense, heavy with meaning. Ella wasn't sure she was ready to understand.

Through the windows, the afternoon light was beginning its slow descent toward evening, painting the lake in shades of silver and purple.

"What if I mess it up?" The question slipped out before she could stop it. "What if I'm not... enough? Sarah spent sixty years learning this place. I've been here three days and I've already had one appliance rebellion." And one impossible jewelry manifestation.

Mrs. Frankl's expression softened, the stern lines of her face rearranging into something that might almost be called maternal. "Sarah didn't start knowing everything either. She was twenty-five when she inherited this place, younger than you are now. Terrified, if I'm being honest."

"You knew her then?"

"Of course."

A memory skittered through Ella's mind. "Stop filling her head with nonsense," Mom's voice, sharp with old anger. "She has to learn to live in the real world."

The tea had been steeping while they talked, and now Mrs. Frankl poured it into delicate china cups painted with tiny forget-me-nots. The scent that rose with the steam was unlike anything Ella had experienced —warm and complex, carrying notes of jasmine and honey and something that tasted like memory itself.

"Try it," Mrs. Frankl said, offering her a cup.

Ella accepted the delicate china, surprised by its warmth against her palms. The first sip was revelation—not just tea but comfort distilled, like every perfect afternoon of her childhood wrapped in liquid form.

"This is incredible. What's in it?"

"Love, mostly. Time. Patience. A little magic for flavor." Mrs. Frankl sat gracefully in the leather chair, sipped her own tea, watched Ella over the rim. "The secret isn't in the blend, child. It's in the intention."

"Intention?"

"Sarah used to say that every cup of tea is a conversation. Between the person pouring and the person receiving. Between what was and what could be. The inn just... amplifies the conversation."

As if summoned by her words, voices drifted in from the lobby. A young couple, from the sound of it, their conversation stilted, nervous.

"Shall we practice?" Mrs. Frankl stood, gathering the tea service. "The inn seems to have provided students."

The tea room occupied the space between on the other side of the kitchen from the dining room. A cozy alcove, tucked next to the turret room, it was furnished with small round tables with linen and lace tablecloths and mismatched chairs that somehow achieved perfect harmony. Late afternoon light filtered through sheer curtains, casting patterns of shadow and warmth across the polished wood floor.

The young couple sat at the table by the window—she was probably mid-twenties with nervous hands and a smile that kept flickering on and off like a faulty bulb. He looked like he'd rather be anywhere else, checking his phone every thirty seconds and drumming his fingers against his coffee cup.

"Classic first date disaster," Mrs. Frankl murmured, setting up the tea service at the old-fashioned sideboard against the wall. on the white marble counter. "Online match, probably. High expectations, no chemistry, both wondering how to escape gracefully."

"How can you tell all that?"

"Forty years of watching people. Plus she's stopped trying to maintain the conversation one-sided and he's sitting at an angle that allows quick access to the exit." Mrs. Frankl measured tea leaves into a pot with surgical precision. "They need Courage and Truth. With a dash of Laughter."

"Those are actual tea blends?"

"Everything is actual if you believe in it strongly enough." Mrs. Frankl poured hot water over the leaves, and the scent that rose was warm and spicy with an undercurrent of mischief. "Now, the proper approach is to offer the service, explain the blends, and let them choose. But sometimes..."

She lifted the teapot, and as the aromatic steam curled upward, something impossible happened.

The other teapots in the room—decorative pieces arranged on shelves and window sills—began to sing.

Not whistling. Singing. A harmonious hum that started low and rose in pitch, each pot contributing its own note to create a melody that sounded like welcome, like coming home, like the musical equivalent of a warm hug.

The young couple's stuttering conversation stopped mid-sentence. They looked around, bewildered but not frightened, as the gentle melody continued to weave through the air.

"What..." the young woman began, then stopped, her hand reaching across the table to touch her date's wrist. "Do you hear that?"

"Yeah." His voice was softer than it had been, the defensive edge gone. "It's beautiful."

Mrs. Frankl moved to their table as if nothing extraordinary was happening and set down the fresh pot and two clean cups.

"Afternoon tea?" she offered. "It's our specialty blend."

The couple exchanged glances, and something had

shifted in the space between them. The nervous energy had transmuted into curiosity, anticipation.

"Please," the young woman said. "I'm Sarah, by the way. And this is Mike."

"Sarah," Mrs. Frankl repeated. "Welcome."

As she poured the tea, the singing teapots gradually quieted, their melody fading to a gentle hum. The couple's body language transformed. Shoulders relaxed. Smiles became genuine. Mike actually put his phone face-down on the table.

"So," Sarah said, accepting her cup with both hands, "I have to ask—do you actually like hiking, or was that just your profile talking?"

Mike's laugh was surprised and genuine. "Man, no. I hate hiking. But you said you loved it, and I thought maybe I could learn to like it maybe."

"I lied about the hiking," Sarah confessed, grinning. "I'm terrified of bears. And bugs. And camping in general."

"Wonderful." Mike leaned forward, suddenly animated. "Want to know what I actually love? Bookstores. Old movies. Making pasta from scratch. Really nerdy stuff."

"I love nerdy stuff," Sarah said softly. "Tell me about the pasta."

Ella watched, transfixed, as two strangers became two people discovering they might actually like each other. The tea—or whatever Mrs. Frankl had put in that pot—seemed to have dissolved their masks.

"How?" she whispered to Mrs. Frankl, who was cleaning up the preparation area with studied nonchalance.

"Good tea. Proper setting. A little help from the inn." The older woman's voice was matter-of-fact, but her eyes were bright with satisfaction. "People want to be real, Ella. They just need permission."

The front door chimed, and familiar footsteps crossed the lobby. Liam appeared in the tea room doorway, tall and blond and carrying a beltful of tools.

"The radiator was acting up?" His gaze swept the room, taking in the cozy scene, the couple now deep in animated conversation, the lingering scent of impossible tea.

"Just temperamental," Mrs. Frankl replied smoothly. "Like most things around here."

Liam knelt beside the cast-iron radiator in the corner. The also had heat pumps and solar panels, but somehow all those renovations had missed this room. Ella noticed his attention wasn't entirely on his work. She watched him watch Sarah and Mike, saw the exact moment his skeptical expression began to soften.

Because this wasn't just conversation anymore. It was connection, real and visible and transformative. Mike was describing his grandmother's recipe for gnocchi with his whole body, hands shaping pasta in the air. Sarah was leaning forward, chin propped on her palm, eyes bright with genuine interest.

"I could teach you," Mike was saying. "The gnocchi, I mean. If you wanted to learn."

"I'd like that," Sarah replied. "I'd really like that."

"Everything seems fine here," Liam said quietly, straightening up. But he wasn't looking at the radiator.

Mrs. Frankl pulled a quilted cover over the tea service. "Some people need a little help remembering they're worth loving."

Liam's gaze shifted to Ella, something unreadable in his blue eyes. "Is that what your tea does? Helps people remember?"

"Among other things." Mrs. Frankl paused, studying both of them with sharp attention. "It's very good at finding what people need, even when they don't know themselves. Or refuse to know." She bustled out the door, a woman who enjoyed having the last word.

Her words hung in the air like a challenge. Ella felt heat rise in her cheeks under Liam's steady gaze, hyper-aware of the space between them, the way her pulse quickened when he looked at her like that.

"I should get back to—" she started.

"Wait." Liam caught her wrist gently, his thumb finding her pulse point. His warmth swept over her like a fleece blanket. "Are you okay? That was... intense."

"Singing teapots, Liam. The teapots were harmonizing." She laughed, but it came out shaky. "How is any of this okay?"

"Hey." He stepped closer, his hand sliding down to interlace their fingers. "Remember what I said about believing?"

"That you're running out of explanations?"

"That some things can't be understood. Only felt." His free hand came up to cup her cheek, thumb brushing across her cheekbone. "Like this."

The air between them crackled. Ella's breath caught as Liam leaned closer, his intent clear in the way his gaze dropped to her lips. The lingering scent of honey and jasmine wrapped around them like a blessing. She found herself rising on her toes to meet him—

"Somebody called Anshultz just phoned!" Cordelia called from the lobby. "Six guests, no reservation, ten minutes out!"

Liam's forehead dropped to rest against hers. "The inn's timing needs work," he murmured.

"The inn's not the only one," she whispered back, but she was smiling.

"The preparations for tomorrow," Mrs. Frankl interrupted smoothly. "Sunday brunch is always busy. You'll want to be ready."

"Right. Brunch." Ella gathered her scattered thoughts with effort. "More cooking lessons?"

"More everything lessons." Mrs. Frankl's smile held promise and threat in equal measure.

As they prepared to leave the tea room, Sarah called out, "Excuse me? The tea—what kind was it? I've never had anything like it."

Mrs. Frankl paused, considering. "Truth and Courage, dear. With a touch of Possibility."

"Is it for sale? I'd love to take some home."

"I'm sorry, but that particular blend only works here." Mrs. Frankl's voice was gentle but firm. "But you're welcome to come back anytime you need reminding of who you really are."

Mike and Sarah exchanged glances full of promise.

"We'll definitely be back," Mike said.

On the way to the kitchen, Ella's phone buzzed again. Another text from Chicago, another reminder of the life waiting for her return.

She ignored it.

Chapter Six

After coming home from another pointless visit to the inn and its lovely new innkeeper, Liam spent Saturday evening trying to fix things that weren't broken.

First, the perfectly functional kitchen faucet in his cottage, which he disassembled and reassembled completely before admitting it had never needed his attention. Then the back porch step that had been solid for three years but suddenly seemed to require extensive examination. Finally, the truck's engine, which purred like a contented cat but still found itself subjected to an oil change that wasn't due for another thousand miles.

None of it helped him stop thinking about teapots that sang in harmony.

By Sunday morning, he'd run out of things to needlessly repair and found himself staring at his coffee maker—a sensible, silent machine that had never once expressed an opinion about his romantic life—with something approaching suspicion.

"Just make coffee," he told it. "No editorials."

It complied without commentary, which should have been reassuring but somehow felt like a personal failing.

The drive to Harbor & Home Hardware gave him a hilltop view of the inn, and he found himself slowing despite his better judgment. The morning light painted the Victorian silhouette in shades of pearl and promise, smoke curling from the kitchen chimney suggesting breakfast service was already underway. For just a moment, he thought he could smell cinnamon and vanilla carried on the lake breeze.

Impossible, of course. He was a quarter mile away with his windows up.

The hardware store sat on Harbor Street's busiest corner like a lighthouse of practicality in a sea of boutique shops that catered to summer tourists. Three generations of Carters had built it into exactly what a hardware store should be—functional, honest, and utterly without pretense. The weathered cedar siding had aged to silver-grey, and the hand-painted sign still bore his grandfather's careful lettering: "Harbor &

Home Hardware - If We Don't Have It, You Don't Need It."

Liam parked in his usual spot behind the building, breathing in the familiar cocktail of scents that meant home. Motor oil and metal shavings. The sharp bite of paint thinner mixed with the earthy smell of potting soil from the garden center. Sawdust and WD-40 and that particular metallic tang that came from thousands of nails, screws, and bolts waiting to hold things together.

The back door opened onto the stockroom, where towers of boxes rose toward water-stained ceiling tiles and fluorescent lights hummed their eternal tune. Here, everything had its place in a system that made sense only to family—paint supplies stacked next to plumbing fittings, extension cords coiled beside bags of road salt left over from last winter. The concrete floor, polished smooth by decades of work boots, felt solid and real beneath his feet.

Here, a wrench was just a wrench. Pipes were meant to carry water, not somehow manifest wedding rings from distant cities. Coffee makers brewed coffee without editorial comment on their owner's abilities.

Walking into the main store always felt like stepping into his grandfather's embrace. Narrow aisles stretched between towering shelves packed with the accumulated necessities of small-town life. Garden hoses coiled beside snow shovels. Fishing tackle shared space with canning supplies. The scent of leather work gloves mixed with the metallic bite of chain and the sweet scent of wood stain.

His boots echoed on the worn linoleum—practical brown speckled with gold, chosen for its ability to hide dirt and last forever. The sound was different from the inn's musical floorboards, more honest somehow. These floors didn't sing or creak with opinions. They simply held their ground, year after year, supporting the weight of people solving practical problems with practical solutions.

Liam breathed deeper, letting the familiar atmosphere settle into his bones. This was his world—predictable, logical, governed by the immutable laws of physics and basic economics. A place where cause followed effect, where problems had solutions you could hold in your hands, where magic was just a word people used for things they didn't understand yet.

Standing among the fertilizer spreaders and socket wrench sets, surrounded by the accumulated wisdom of three generations of practical people, he almost managed to convince himself that singing teapots were just a hallucination brought on by too little sleep and too much coffee.

Almost.

"About time," his sister Katie called from behind the paint counter, where she was mixing a custom color for

Mrs. Kowalski. His former third-grade teacher must have fallen out of love with the puce they'd painted her kitchen in last year. Two years ago? So he should pencil that project in, soon by the looks of it. Katie probably already on the family's online calendar, the one Liam turned all the notifications off of. The mechanical whir of the paint mixer filled the air, along with the sharp chemical scent of latex and tinting compounds.

"Mom's been brewing gossip since she opened," Katie said.

"Morning to you too." Liam headed for the coffee station in the back—a folding table wedged between the electrical supplies and a display of work gloves, holding a coffee maker that was older than he was and a box of generic creamer packets. His father's concession to modern retail demands had been grudging at best. The coffee was strong enough to strip paint and tasted like it had been brewing since the Reagan administration, but it was excellent at caffeine delivery. "And it's not gossip if it's business-related."

"Everything's business-related when it involves the Thompson girl," Katie shot back, grinning. "Especially when my brother's been making mysterious repair runs every day since she arrived."

Through the stockroom door, he could hear his mother's voice mixing with another customer's—Doc Hendricks, probably, based on the particular rhythm of scandalous speculation that characterized her conversations.

"—saw him there three times this week alone," his mother was saying. "And you know the inn's perfectly maintained. Sarah saw to that before she passed."

"Maybe he's being neighborly," Doc Hendricks suggested with the tone of someone who absolutely didn't believe her own words.

"We did raise that boy to be helpful," his mother agreed, "but we also raised him to be practical. And there's nothing practical about visiting a functioning property every day unless..."

"Unless what, Mom?" Liam stepped into the stockroom, coffee in hand and resignation in his voice.

His mother—a woman who'd never met a conversation she couldn't steer toward her own agenda—beamed at him with the particular satisfaction of a hunter who'd just watched her prey walk into the trap. Like Katie, she was tall, strong, and sharper than a new razor.

"Unless you've taken a professional interest in the new owner," she finished smoothly. "How is she settling in, by the way? Poor thing, inheriting all that responsibility."

"She's managing fine." Liam kept his voice carefully neutral, but something in his tone must have betrayed him because both women perked up like hunting dogs scenting prey.

"Managing fine," his mother repeated thoughtfully. "That's awfully... diplomatic."

"Accurate."

"Mmm." She exchanged a look with Doc Hendricks that contained decades of maternal intuition and small-town surveillance. The doc, the silver-haired no-nonsense local G.P. who knew everybody's ailments by heart, to the embarrassment of quite a few, took up the charge.

"And what's she like? Personality-wise?" she said.

Liam found himself considering the question more seriously than he'd intended. What was Ella like? Thoughtful, fierce when cornered, gentle with broken things. Beautiful, obviously, but not in the polished, untouchable way of magazine covers—beautiful like sunrise over the lake, natural and warm and somehow essential.

"She's..." He stopped, aware that both women were watching his face with the intensity of scientists observing a particularly interesting specimen. "She's good with people. Learns fast. The staff likes her."

"The staff likes her," his mother said. She tapped her cheek thoughtfully. "That's important. Sarah was very particular about who belonged at that place."

"Everyone belongs somewhere," Doc Hendricks added. "Question is whether they're smart enough to recognize it."

"Some people," his mother said, still watching Liam with laser focus, "take longer than others to figure out where they fit."

The conversation felt increasingly like a chess match where everyone else knew the rules except him. Liam drained his coffee and headed for the door, but his mother's voice stopped him at the threshold.

"You know," she said casually, "your grandfather always said the inn would know when it found its next keeper. Said there were signs."

"What kind of signs?"

"Oh, the usual. Impossible becoming possible. Lost items finding their way home. The lynx walking again." Her voice held the particular tone she'd used when he was small and she was telling him stories that might or might not be true. "He claimed he heard its whispers the night he met your grandmother. Led her right to him in that terrible storm."

Doc Hendricks nodded. "My mother told similar stories. Said the lynx guided lovers together when the time was right."

"Folklore," Liam said automatically, but the word tasted strange in his mouth.

"Maybe." His mother's smile was gentle but knowing. "But your grandfather was a practical man, son. Not given to flights of fancy. When he said the lynx whispered directions to love, he meant it literally."

"And you believed him?"

"I believed him enough to pay attention when she said you had the gift too." She moved closer, studying his face with maternal precision. "You used to hear things, remember? Used to leave cookies on the porch for something you swore was watching from the dunes."

The memory hit him like cold water—himself at six or seven, sneaking oatmeal cookies from the jar and arranging them in careful patterns on the back steps. Listening for sounds that weren't quite wind, watching for movements that weren't quite shadows. The absolute certainty that something ancient and protective was keeping watch over their family, over the whole town.

"I was a kid," he said, but his voice lacked conviction. "Kids believe in all sorts of things."

"Kids believe in what adults have forgotten how to see." His mother reached out, squeezing his shoulder with callused hands that smelled of garden soil and mint. "Maybe it's time to remember."

After that, he couldn't concentrate on anything. He completed his Sunday errands on autopilot—paying the store's weekly bills, groceries, a stop at the post office where Mrs. Patterson asked pointed questions about his sudden interest in inn maintenance—but his mind kept drifting to childhood memories he'd buried under years of adult rationality.

The cookies on the porch. The dreams of golden

eyes watching from the darkness. His grandfather's stories about rooms that matched themselves to guests' hearts, about lovers who met in impossible ways, about a lynx that walked between worlds to protect what mattered most.

When had he stopped believing? Gradually, probably, the way childhood magic always faded—replaced by homework and heartbreak and the grinding reality of growing up in a small town where escape felt more appealing than acceptance.

Amanda's leaving hadn't helped. She'd been his first serious girlfriend, the girl he'd thought he'd marry, until she'd announced her acceptance to college three states away and her complete lack of interest in small-town limitations. He'd offered to follow, to build something new somewhere else, but she'd looked at him with something dangerously close to pity.

"You belong here, Liam," she'd said. "Your roots go too deep to transplant. But mine were always shallow."

Maybe that's when he'd stopped listening for whispers on the wind. When believing in magic felt too much like believing in things that would eventually leave.

Ella wasn't any different. Was she? She'd inherited the inn, inherited the responsibility and the impossible magic that came with it. She couldn't just walk away from that.

Could she?

The thought followed him through Sunday afternoon and into evening, through a dinner he barely tasted and a shower that did nothing to wash away his growing certainty that something fundamental was shifting in his carefully ordered world.

He fell asleep thinking about teapots that sang and wedding rings that traveled across states and the way Ella's eyes had widened when she'd realized the impossible was becoming routine.

He dreamed of golden eyes.

They watched him from the dunes, patient and ancient and achingly familiar. The lynx—because it was definitely the lynx, he knew that with dream-logic certainty—sat poised on the highest peak of sand, silhouetted against a sky full of stars that pulsed like heartbeats.

In the dream, he stood on the beach below, seven years old, wearing his grandfather's giant pea coat. The sand was warm beneath his bare feet despite the autumn night, and the air hummed with possibility.

What do you want from me? he asked.

The scene shifted, and he was in the inn's turret room, watching Ella sleep in the starlight. Her hair spread across the pillow like spilled honey, and her face held the soft vulnerability of someone finally at peace. The room hummed around her, protective and welcoming, and he understood with crystalline clarity that this was where she belonged.

Where they both belonged.

Help her remember, the lynx whispered. Remember she's home.

But the dream was already fading, golden eyes dissolving into morning light as his alarm clock insisted on the return of ordinary time.

Liam woke with the taste of wind in his mouth and the absolute certainty that he'd experienced something more than mere dreaming. The bedroom felt different— charged with the same energy he'd felt in the inn, alive with possibilities he couldn't name.

He sat up, running hands through his hair, and froze.

Sand.

Fine, golden sand scattered across his sheets, his pillowcase, the floor beside his bed. Not much—just enough to be unmistakable, impossible, and utterly real.

He lived in the woods, more than a mile from the nearest beach. His cottage sat on solid ground with hardwood floors and windows that had been closed all night. There was no logical way for dune sand to appear in his bedroom.

Unless logic wasn't the right tool for understanding what was happening to his life.

Liam gathered the sand in his palm, feeling its

familiar grit against his skin. It was warm, as if it had been sitting in sunshine despite the early morning hour. As if it had been carried from the dunes not by wind or accident, but by intention.

By magic.

Standing there in his bedroom, holding impossible evidence of forces he'd spent twenty years dismissing, Liam made a decision that would have terrified his rational adult self.

He chose to believe.

The lynx had walked in his dreams, had spoken in whispers older than memory, had left sand like bread-crumbs leading back to faith he'd abandoned.

And Ella—beautiful, bewildered Ella—was at the center of it all.

He dressed quickly, pocketing the sand with the solemnity of someone accepting a sacred trust. Outside, the morning air carried the scent of autumn leaves and frost. In the distance, the inn waited with all its impossible promises.

Chapter Seven

The reservation system had officially declared war on logic.

Ella sat in Sarah's office chair at 7 PM on Monday, staring at the old-fashioned computer screen with the particular exhaustion that came from fighting technology that had developed opinions. For the third time that afternoon, the system had moved a couple from Chicago from the Harbor Master's Room to the Lighthouse Keeper's Room. Every time she switched it back, citing their original request for "something nautical but quiet," the computer waited exactly seventeen minutes before changing the assignment again.

"This is insane," she muttered, clicking through screens that seemed to rearrange themselves when she wasn't looking. "Computer systems don't have preferences."

The ancient monitor—a boxy beige monument to 1990s optimism—flickered once, as if in disagreement.

She'd been trying to create order from the inn's booking chaos for two hours. A woman from Cincinnati had been moved from the Dune Walker's Room to the Rose Suite and back again four times. Another couple arriving next week had somehow been assigned to three different rooms simultaneously. And no matter what she did, one unfortunate couple, now exes but returning for a big family reunion, kept ending up on the same floor, often in adjoining rooms.

"Subtle," she told the screen. "Really subtle."

The lights flickered in response.

Then they went out entirely.

Ella sat in sudden darkness, the computer screen fading to black with a electronic sigh that sounded almost satisfied. Outside, she could hear surprised voices from the tea room, the clatter of cups being set down with more force than usual.

"Perfect," she said to the darkness. "Just perfect."

She fumbled for the flashlight Sarah kept in the desk drawer, pushed away from the cranky computer and made her way to the lobby. The dusk filtering through the tall windows provided plenty of illumination, but shadows gathered in corners like curious neighbors waiting for gossip.

The sand globe sat serene on its pedestal. It wasn't swirling, exactly. More like glittering. Watching.

Staccato voices drifted down from the second floor—Marcus and Kelsey, probably wondering about the power outage. She should check on them, make sure they had candles or alternative lighting. Good innkeeper behavior. Professional host duties.

She climbed the stairs. In the semi-darkness, the familiar creaks seemed more musical; the shadows shifted in ways that suggested movement just beyond her peripheral vision. The second floor hallway stretched before her, lit only by the pale rectangle of the window at the far end.

"Dr. Chen? Kelsey?" she called softly. "Everything okay up here?"

Kelsey came right out of her room, camera in hand.

"I'm fine," Marcus's voice came from the Lighthouse Keeper's Room, muffled but clearly audible. "Just... the door seems to be stuck."

Of course it was.

Ella approached the room. The brass nameplate beside the door gleamed in her flashlight beam.

"Step back from the door," she called, setting her shoulder against the heavy oak. The inn's doors were solid, built to last, and this one had never given anyone trouble before. She pushed, then tried lifting the handle while turning it. Nothing.

"It doesn't sound locked," Kelsey's voice was closer to the door now, tinged with amusement rather than concern. "It just... won't open. Like something's holding it shut."

Ella tried the handle again, this time with a firm "please" added under her breath.

The door swung open so suddenly she nearly fell forward into the room.

"Sorry about that," Ella said, though she wasn't entirely sure what she was apologizing for. "Sometimes the old doors—"

Light exploded across the room.

Not electric light, but something far more dramatic —a brilliant white beam that swept through the windows and transformed the entire space into something from a maritime dream. The lighthouse, the actual lighthouse on the distant spit of land to the south that had been dead for fifty years, was somehow, impossibly, operational.

In that spectacular illumination, Ella saw the Lighthouse Keeper's Room as it was meant to be seen.

The walls, painted in deep navy blue with white trim, seemed to glow with captured starlight. Brass fixtures that had merely gleamed in artificial light now blazed like captured suns. The bed, dressed in crisp white linens with a navy wool blanket folded at the foot, looked like something from a ship captain's quarters. Antique nautical charts lined the walls, their coastlines and depth measurements suddenly clear and purposeful in the sweeping light.

The massive window seat followed follow the room's unique architecture. Deep cushions in storm-blue fabric invited long conversations, while small brass lamps mounted on the wall provided reading light for those drawn to watch the water. A telescope stood in the corner, its brass fittings reflecting the lighthouse beam like a signal mirror.

"Wow," Kelsey said from the hallway. "Mind if I take some photos your room?" That sweep of light changes everything."

"Sure," Marcus said, clearly more interested in getting back to his medical journals than making conversation.

The lighthouse beam swept across the room, big and bright and completely impossible.

Kelsey gasped, lifting her camera. "Incredible! The way the light transforms the space, even the colors. Do you mind if I take a few shots with you in frame? For scale?"

"I'd rather not," Marcus said politely. He pushed back his wire-rimmed glasses, juggling a stack of journals in the crook of his other arm. "But feel free to use the room. I was actually planning to head over to the library to read."

Both women watched him head down the hall away from the main stairs, towards the library room at the end of the hall.

"Okaaay," Kelsey said, and returned to her photo taking.

Ella fled down to the lobby, pulse racing, thoughts scattered like startled birds. This was getting out of hand. First the wedding ring, then the singing teapots, now defunct lighthouses blazing to life. How was she supposed to run a business when the business insisted on defying the basic laws of physics?

Her phone chirped. Email. Chicago. Her real life. The quarterly reports that needed filing, the meetings she was missing, the promotion that hinged on her bringing back a professional assessment of this property.

She pulled her phone out of her pocket.

Subject: RE: RE: Time-Sensitive

No response? This isn't like you. The Pinnacle people want to move fast. They're talking February closing if the numbers work. That's a $2M project you'd be lead on. Career-making stuff.

If you can't handle a simple assessment, maybe you're not ready for senior positions.

Expecting your call Monday AM.

Ella stared at the phone through three more rings,

knowing she should answer, knowing Markie's patience was wearing thin. On the fourth ring, a text popped up:

I can see you're declining my calls. Very professional. Richard from Pinnacle is flying to Chicago Thursday. He wants YOU to present the Michigan property. Don't blow this.

The sand globe chimed once, softly. When she glanced at it, the golden sand had formed a new shape—a small girl with wild curls, dancing in what looked like a garden, arms spread wide to embrace the whole world.

It was late.

She'd email Markie tomorrow.

Maybe.

The lights throughout the lobby brightened slowly in what felt impossibly like agreement. Or the power coming back on.

Somewhere upstairs, a door closed with a gentle click—not the slam of rejection but the soft sound of someone settling in for the night.

Chapter Eight

In the dusky, quiet lobby, the front desk beckoned like an anchor in her spinning world. Ella needed information, documentation, some kind of manual that explained how previous owners had managed an inn that seemed to operate more like a fairy tale than a hospitality business.

The desk itself was a masterpiece of nineteenth-century craftsmanship—the top carved from what looked like a single piece of oak, its surface worn smooth by countless hands checking guests in and out. The grain ran in beautiful curved patterns that seemed to flow like water, and the side panels were decorated with subtle carvings of vines and stars. It dominated the lobby's northwest wall, positioned to see both the front door and the stairs, a command center disguised as elegant furniture.

Ella settled into the chair behind it—Sarah's chair, tall as a stool, carved with the same attention to detail as the desk itself. The seat had been shaped by decades of use, conforming to the particular curves of innkeepers who'd sat there morning and evening, welcoming guests and managing the daily mysteries of this place.

The desk's long, shimmering surface held only one of those ancient monitors for reservations and the massive bound register book that held decades of guest signatures. Drawers and cubbyholes filled the space underneath, each sized for specific purposes—registration cards, room keys, stamps, the small items that kept a hotel functioning. Everything had its place in a system refined by generations of women who'd understood that organization was the foundation of hospitality.

But it was the hidden spaces that made the desk special. Ella had discovered some of them already—the secret compartment behind the bottom drawer, the panel that slid aside to reveal a safe for storing valuable items.

Now, running her hands along the carved edges with desperate hope, she found another.

A gentle pressure on a carved star caused a section of the left support panel to slide aside, revealing a tall, deep, compartment. Inside, wrapped in oiled cloth and scented faintly of lavender, were guest books.

Ella lifted the first volume with trembling hands. The leather cover was soft with age, warm to the touch as if it had been waiting in sunlight rather than darkness. "2020-2025" was written on the first inside page.

She opened it randomly, and Sarah's handwriting leaped off the page. the same careful script that had signed birthday cards and written grocery lists and labeled everything in the inn with quiet precision.

October 15, 2022: The Jacobsen anniversary couple arrived today believing their marriage was over. Forty years, and they could barely look at each other. I put them in separate rooms as requested—he in Harbor Master's, she in the Rose Suite. But the inn knew better. This morning I found them having coffee together in the garden, holding hands like newlyweds. Mrs. J said she'd dreamed of their first date, remembered the boy who'd brought her daisies picked from a highway median because he couldn't afford a bouquet. Mr. J had found those same wildflowers growing impossibly beside his door this morning. The Stargazer Suite is ready for them tonight. Together, as they should be.

Ella's vision blurred. She jumped forward and back with careful fingers, reading entry after entry.

December 3, 2021: Young Dr. Martinez couldn't sleep

—first-year resident, convinced she'd made a terrible mistake choosing medicine. Put her in the Lighthouse Room, knowing what it would do. This morning she told me she'd seen the lighthouse beam sweep across her wall at 3 AM, pointing toward the children's hospital in the distance. "Like a calling," she said. Left with such purpose in her steps.

June 18, 2023: The Bennett family, still shattered from losing their eldest in Afghanistan. Their remaining son, quiet as a ghost. The Blue Room opened for him when it's been locked for months. Inside, he found a baseball glove—exactly like the one his brother had given him, lost in their move. He played catch with his father for the first time in two years.

The entries went on—businessmen who found clarity, artists who rediscovered inspiration, families knit back together by impossible coincidences that weren't coincidences at all. And threaded throughout, mentions of Ella herself:

August 1, 2022 :Ella's birthday today. Twenty-six and probably celebrating in some Chicago high rise. I send my love on the wind and trust it finds her. The Blue Room rattles its doorknob every year on this day—it remembers its favorite guest. Someday she'll come back to open it.

Ella gasped, pressing her hand to her mouth. The Blue Room—her room—had been waiting for her?

She reached for an older volume. Her grandmother's writing was younger here, stronger:

July 4, 2004: Little Ella (age 8) has announced she wants to be "the inn boss" when she grows up. She's made a roster for the chipmunks and is trying to teach them to bring guests their shoes. I haven't the heart to tell her that's not quite how it works. Though knowing this place, perhaps she's onto something...

And then, with shaking fingers, Ella found the entry that broke her:

September 1, 2007: They left today. Patty finally made good on her threats to keep Ella away from "all this nonsense." Twenty years of careful peace shattered because Ella mentioned the lynx at the wrong moment—told her mother about seeing golden eyes in the garden, about the whispers that helped her find lost things. Patricia's face when she realized I'd been "filling her head with the same lies that ruined my childhood." My child looked at me with such anger. And Ella—my bright, magical girl— bewildered as her mother dragged her to the car. The inn mourns with me. Every door hangs crooked. The coffee maker weeps steam. Even the sand globe has gone still. I pray she'll remember. I pray she'll come back. The inn needs her. I need her.

The book slipped from Ella's numb fingers, landing open on the desk. Her shoulders shook with the weight of understanding. All those years of careful distance, of birthday cards acknowledged but visits postponed, of choosing her mother's practical world over her grandmother's magical one—all because she'd mentioned seeing something her mother couldn't accept.

"I'm sorry," she whispered to the empty lobby. "Gran, I'm so sorry."

She reached for another volume, this one from the 1960s, the handwriting different. Sarah's mother?

November 12, 1962: The lynx walked last night. Young Tom Whitmore saw it first, standing in the garden beneath the full moon. Golden eyes like stars, he said, watching the inn as if keeping guard. By morning, three couples had found each other—the Emersons reconciling after months of separation, the shy librarian and the baker's son finally speaking their hearts, and most surprisingly, my own dear Sarah accepting Harold's proposal at last. The lynx knows when love needs a nudge. Mother always said it would return when the inn's magic grew strongest.

More volumes, going back further. Different hands, different eras, but the same truth repeated:

1943: The war has taken so many, but the inn provides comfort. Soldiers on leave find peace here, reminders of what they're fighting for. Last night, Errol Morrison found his mother's rosary on his pillow—the one lost in the bombing of their London home. He wept like a child.

1928: The Stargazer Suite revealed itself today! A hidden door that's never been there before, leading to a round room in the turret. Perfect for the astronomy professor and his new bride.

1901 - First entry in this new century. The old ways are changing, but the inn remains. The native peoples always knew this land was special, "where the spirit of the great lynx dwells," they say. We are merely caretakers.

Generations of women, all documenting the same impossible truths. All believing, serving, protecting this magical place.

She reached for the oldest volume she could find, its leather binding crackling with age. The first entry was dated 1887, written in fading brown ink.

I, Margaret Blackstone, begin this record on the occasion of the opening of this Starlight Arbor Inn. The building sits beside the sacred dune the Anishinaabe people called "Where the Lynx Whispers." They say love spoken here becomes truth, that hearts find their match when the wind carries their wishes to the great lynx's ears. Already, we have seen wonders. Rooms that appear when needed. Guests who find what they thought lost forever. The sand in the great globe—gifted by the tribal elders— moves without touch, showing visions of what may come to pass. My daughters shall inherit this duty, and their daughters after them, for as long as the lynx watches over this land.

Her great-great-great-grandmother. Ella traced the faded words. All of them, here.

Waiting. Expecting she'd return.

As she had.

Footsteps on the porch interrupted her tears. The front door opened, bringing with it the scent of evening air and approaching autumn—and WD-40.

Liam.

His voice carried across the lobby, warm and familiar.

"Seen Marcus and Kelsey? We're headed for the Night Skies tour. Park Service is setting up telescopes at the overlook, and the weather's perfect for—"

He stopped mid-sentence. "Hey," he said softly, crossing to the desk "You okay?"

She gestured helplessly at the books spread across the desk. "I found them. The records—the real ones. Everything Sarah wrote, everything her mother wrote, all of them, all the way back." Her voice cracked. "She wrote about me. Wrote about waiting for me. And I stayed away because my mother said so, and I chose—I chose—"

"Hey." He crossed the lobby in three quick strides, coming around the desk without hesitation. "Hey, it's okay."

"It's not okay." The words tumbled out between fresh tears. "Seventeen years. She waited seventeen years for me to come back, and I let my mother's fear keep me away. Her refusal to believe. I destroyed everything."

Liam knelt beside her chair, his presence solid and warm. His dark eyes were soft with understanding, and when he reached out to brush a tear from her cheek, she didn't pull away.

"You didn't destroy anything," he said gently. "You were a kid. A kid caught between two adults who couldn't agree."

"She loved you," he said simply. "She talked about you constantly. Every achievement, every milestone—she celebrated them all, even from a distance."

"I should have come back sooner. I should have brought her to Chicago, or visited more, or—"

"You're here now." His thumb traced along her cheekbone, gentle and warm. "That's what matters. That's what she wanted."

"She knew I'd come back," Ella whispered, her voice breaking. "But I don't know if I'm meant to run this place or... assess its market value." The words tasted bitter. "My corporate training says document everything, find the flaws, determine fair market price. But this..." She gestured at the books. "How do you put a price on magic?"

Liam's hand found hers among the scattered books, his touch grounding her in the present. Ella turned her hand in his, interlacing their fingers. The gesture felt like a promise, though she wasn't sure of what.

Footsteps on the wide main stairs. Marcus and Kelsey were making their way down. They'd be here in a moment.

But for now, Ella let herself lean into Liam's touch. She let herself believe.

"The lighthouse turned on," she whispered. "When they kissed. It actually turned on."

Liam's smile was soft and knowing. "Not too subtle, eh?"

Marcus and Kelsey appeared at the top of the stairs, faces bright. They'd changed clothes again, this time jeans and sweatshirts, or in Kelsey's case, a windbreaker with reflective tape on the back and wrists.

"Ready for some stargazing?" Marcus called down.

"Perfect night for it," Liam replied, standing but not moving away from Ella. "Clear skies, new moon. You'll be able to see the Milky Way."

As the couple descended the stairs, Ella carefully closed the guest books. The magic they contained wasn't something to hide, exactly, but it felt too precious, too personal to share with people who hadn't earned the right to witness it.

"Come with?" Liam asked quietly.

The thought was too much. She needed hot tea and a fire in the fireplace.

"Next time," Ella said.

"You'll be okay?"

She looked around the lobby—at the sand globe swirling gently in its eternal patterns, at the desk that had held the secrets of generations, at the stairs that led to rooms where unexpected things happened daily.

Her inheritance, her responsibility, her calling.

"Yes" she said, and meant it.

Chapter Nine

The first Saturday in October dawned crisp with promise, the kind of day that made you believe autumn was the most beautiful season ever invented. Ella stood on the inn's front porch, breathing in air that tasted of woodsmoke and fallen leaves, watching Mrs. Frankl load the last of their festival supplies into her practical blue sedan.

"You're sure about this?" Ella asked for the third time, adjusting Sarah's cardigan against the morning chill. "I could just write a check to the festival committee and call it community support."

Mrs. Frankl straightened from arranging the covered dishes in her backseat, fixing Ella with the look she probably used to discipline unruly guests. "Your grandmother participated in every Green Arbor festival for sixty years. Missing the first one after her death would send entirely the wrong message."

"But what if—"

"What if the townspeople discover you're exactly who this place has been waiting for?" Mrs. Frankl's smile was warm but implacable. "What a terrible tragedy that would be."

The festival had been in preparation all week—banners strung between lampposts, shop windows decorated with corn stalks and carved pumpkins, the particular energy that came when a small town decided to celebrate itself. From the inn's hilltop perch, Ella had watched the activity like a nervous observer, safe in her distance from community expectations.

Today, there was nowhere to hide.

Mrs. Frankl slid into the driver's seat—all the other seats taken by supplies—and turned the key in an engine that started with suspicious eagerness. "I'll meet you at the booth. The sisters are already down there, claiming our spot and terrifying anyone who might consider competing with our baked goods."

"You mean Agnes, Beatrice, and Cordelia are already—"

"Defending your honor, yes." Mrs. Frankl's expression softened slightly. "They've been planning this for weeks, dear. Don't disappoint them."

The sedan pulled away with a cheerful honk, leaving

Ella alone with her nerves and the quarter-mile downhill walk that would introduce her to Green Arbor as a resident rather than a visitor.

She'd driven through the town countless times as a child, but walking was different. Walking meant you belonged to the place, were part of its daily rhythm instead of just passing through. Walking meant people could see you, evaluate you, decide whether you fit into the carefully woven fabric of their community.

When Ella took her walks, they were usually away from town, along the ridge of the dunes. The closest dune trail started right behind the inn. In this season, she saw hardly anyone on the paths. Just tourists.

The inn's driveway curved down to meet Main Street, Green Arbor's main artery. Across the street stretched a neighborhood of Victorian-era homes that had been lovingly maintained by families who understood the value of preservation. Each house told a story—the blue one with the wraparound porch where Mrs. Patterson grew prize-winning roses, the yellow cottage where the Haapalas had raised four children and countless foster cats, the grand dame painted in shades of green and cream that housed three generations of the Morrison family.

Maples lined the street, their leaves a symphony of gold and scarlet that crunched pleasantly underfoot. The morning sun filtered through the now-spare canopy, creating a natural cathedral of light and shadow.

As she walked the two blocks into town, Ella could hear the festival coming to life—the distant sound of booths being assembled, the cheerful chaos of volunteers calling instructions to each other, the particular energy that preceded any good small-town celebration. The scent of cinnamon and apple cider drifted on the breeze, mixed with woodsmoke from the warming fires that would anchor the food court.

Here along Main stretched businesses that had weathered decades of economic storms by serving both locals and the steady stream of tourists drawn to the lake and dunes. This morning, it buzzed with pre-festival energy.

Mama Lynx Creamery had draped its storefront in orange and gold bunting, with a chalkboard sign promising "Pumpkin Spice Ice Cream - Limited Edition!" The bookstore—Pages & Sage, according to the hand-lettered sign—displayed autumn-themed titles in its picture window, while someone inside arranged what looked like a poetry reading corner with vintage armchairs and a small microphone.

Harbor & Home Hardware anchored the next corner, its practical facade softened by planters full of orange and yellow mums. Through the wide windows, Ella could see people moving around inside—probably the Carter family preparing for their own festival booth.

Next block, the businesses grew more tourist-oriented as she walked—gift shops with windows full of lynx-themed merchandise, a gallery featuring local landscape photography, a coffee roastery that perfumed the air with the promise of caffeine sophistication. But underneath the visitor appeal, she could sense the community that existed year-round, the network of relationships that kept this place alive when the summer crowds departed.

She turned left onto Manitou Street, a long residential lane that dead-ended at the public beach and, this morning, hosted the Green Arbor Fall Festival. The street had been closed to traffic, transformed into a festival ground that stretched from Main Street to the sandy shore of Lake Michigan.

The transformation was remarkable. Booths lined both sides of the narrow street, their colorful awnings and signs creating a temporary marketplace that felt both festive and intimate. At the far end, where the street met the beach sat the Dune's End Restaurant—a weathered building with large windows facing the water and a parking lot that today overflowed more festival booths.

The scent hit her first—cinnamon, vanilla, and warm spices mixing with the crisp lake air. Then the sounds: laughter, conversation, the cheerful chaos of a community celebrating itself. Children ran between booths while their parents browsed handmade crafts and sampled local delicacies. Older couples strolled arm in arm, stopping to chat with vendors they'd known for decades.

This was what she'd been missing from her laser-focused Chicago existence. The sense of belonging to something larger than yourself, of being woven into a quilt of relationships that stretched back generations and forward into an uncertain but hopeful future.

The inn's booth was positioned halfway down the street, strategically placed between the hardware store's display of seasonal tools and the bookstore's collection of local authors. Mrs. Frankl must have arrived first thing to claim such a prime location—close enough to the action to draw foot traffic, but with enough space for people to linger and sample their offerings.

Agnes, Beatrice, and Cordelia had transformed the simple blue-tented canopy into something that looked like it belonged in a fairy tale. White tablecloths covered folding tables, held down against the lake breeze by small pumpkins and gourds that seemed to glow with internal light. Handmade signs in elegant script announced "Starlight Arbor Inn - Where Love Finds Its Home" and "Taste the Magic - Sarah's Famous Cinnamon Treats."

But it was what sat in the center of the main table that made Ella's heart skip.

The sand globe. The massive, supposedly immovable sand globe that had held court in the inn's lobby for over a century. It sat serenely on a specially prepared stand, its golden sand swirling in lazy spirals while the tiny lynx figure seemed to watch the passing crowd with gemstone eyes.

"How?" Ella demanded as she approached the booth.

"Good morning to you too, dear," Cordelia chirped, arranging what looked like several dozen individually wrapped cinnamon rolls in a pattern that somehow managed to be both artistic and appetizing.

"The sand globe. How is it here?"

"Dolly," Agnes said matter-of-factly, not looking up from her arrangement of promotional materials. "Mrs. Frankl brought the hardware store's furniture dolly. Rolled it right out like it wanted to come to the festival."

"It must weigh a hundred pounds. It's never been moved—"

"Moved easily enough this morning," Beatrice interrupted, her tone suggesting that questioning the inn's decisions was both futile and slightly rude. "Seemed eager to be here, actually. Almost rolled itself onto the dolly."

Ella stared at the globe, which continued its gentle

swirling as if attending festivals was the most natural thing in the world. A small crowd was already gathering around it, drawn by its hypnotic movement and the way the sunlight caught the golden sand.

"Welcome to your first Green Arbor festival," Mrs. Frankl's voice came from behind her. The older woman had returned from parking at the grocery store across Main. She carried an open thermos that smelled like heaven and wore an expression of quiet satisfaction. "How does it feel to be part of the community?"

Before Ella could answer, a warm voice called out from the booth next door.

"You must be Ella Thompson!"

She turned to find a woman about her own age approaching with a wide smile and paint-stained hands. Tall and lean with sandy brown hair pulled back in a practical ponytail, she moved with the easy confidence of someone completely comfortable in her own skin.

"Katie Carter," the woman said, extending her hand. "Liam's sister. We've been looking forward to meeting you properly."

"Oh! Katie." Ella accepted the handshake, noting the calluses that spoke of physical work and the warmth that suggested genuine friendliness rather than mere politeness. "Your brother's been incredibly helpful with the inn."

"Helpful," Katie repeated with a knowing grin. "That's one word for it."

From the hardware store booth, a well-constructed bamboo fortress, an older woman emerged carrying a short display rack of dried herbs. This had to be Margaret Carter—Liam's mother. She was shorter than Katie but moved with the same easy confidence, silver hair neatly arranged and eyes that missed nothing.

"Miss Thompson," she said warmly, setting down her tray to offer both hands in greeting. "I'm Margaret Carter. We're so glad you're here."

The gesture was unexpectedly maternal, the kind of welcome that suggested Ella had already been accepted rather than merely tolerated. "Please, call me Ella. And thank you—everyone's been so kind."

"Small towns take care of their own," Margaret Carter said. "And you're definitely one of ours now."

Ella wasn't quite sure what to say to that. Guilt slithered up her spine. She was planning to sell the inn. Wasn't she?

The conversation was interrupted by excited murmurs from a family around the sand globe. Ella turned to see a young girl pointing and exclaiming, her face lit with wonder and delight.

"Lookit!" she was showing her mother. "Lighthouse!"

Ella peered closer, and gasped. The sand inside the

globe was indeed forming shapes—not random swirls but recognizable images. The lighthouse, the inn itself perched on its hill, even what looked like the festival street with its colorful booths.

"Impossible," she breathed.

"Impossible or not," Mrs. Carter said with a chuckle, "it's certainly good for business. Look at that crowd."

She was right. Word was spreading through the festival, drawing people from other booths to witness the sand globe's performance.

"Go ahead and send 'em over to us when you're through with them," Mrs. Carter said, heading back to her own booth with a wave.

Children pressed close to the table, their faces bright with wonder, while adults stood transfixed by the continuously changing scenes.

"Does it always do that?" a teenager asked, pointing at the globe.

Agnes, Beatrice, and Cordelia exchanged one of their telepathic looks.

"Only when it has something to show," Agnes said mysteriously.

"Like what?" the girl persisted.

"Like the magic that happens when people find where they belong," Cordelia added with a gentle smile.

Ella's stomach fell. This was exactly what she'd been

afraid of—the inn's magic becoming a public spectacle, turning their booth into a curiosity rather than a legitimate business promotion.

But as she watched the crowd, she realized something else was happening. People weren't pointing and laughing at the impossible sand globe. They were smiling, sharing stories, connecting with each other over the shared experience of witnessing something wonderful.

"My grandmother met my grandfather here in Green Arbor," a man was telling his grandson. "Always said there was something special about this place."

"I proposed to my wife on that beach," another visitor added, gesturing toward the lake. "Twenty-five years ago next month."

The sand globe seemed to respond to these stories, its movements becoming more elaborate, showing scenes that looked suspiciously like couples walking hand in hand along the shore, children building sandcastles, families gathering around bonfires.

"It's reading the crowd," Ella whispered to Mrs. Frankl. "Showing them what they want to see."

"Showing them what's important," Mrs. Frankl said. "Love, family, connection. The things this place has always nurtured."

A commotion at the promotional materials table drew Ella's attention. A middle-aged couple was reading one of the inn's brochures with expressions of delighted confusion.

"Honey, take a look at this," the woman was saying to her husband. "The room descriptions keep changing."

Ella hurried over to see what they meant, her heart sinking as she anticipated another magical malfunction. Sure enough, the carefully crafted brochures—which should have contained practical information about amenities and rates—were transforming before her eyes.

Where "Queen bed, private bath, lake view" should have appeared, the text now read: "Where hearts find harbor after storms of doubt."

The Rose Suite's description had become: "Love blooms eternal in this garden of second chances."

The Stargazer Suite's practical bullet points had transformed into: "Dance with destiny under stars that remember every whispered promise."

This was a disaster.

Or not. Ella took another look at the couple's faces. They weren't confused or concerned. They were enchanted.

"We have to stay here," the woman said to her husband. "Listen to this description of the Rose Suite: 'Where thorns of past hurts become the stems that support new growth.'" Her eyes were bright with tears. "It's like it knows we're working things out."

"How much for the Rose Suite?" the husband asked, pulling out his wallet with the eagerness of someone who'd found exactly what he'd been looking for.

Ella's mouth opened and closed soundlessly.

"Two nights, continental breakfast included," Mrs. Frankl said smoothly, appearing at Ella's elbow with a tablet that had their reservation app on it. "And complimentary afternoon tea service."

As Mrs. Frankl processed the booking, Ella noticed more people gathered around the sample table where Cordelia was offering "tastes of Sarah's famous treats." Something impossible was happening there too.

"Are these..." Ella began, watching people's faces light up as they tried the samples.

"Sarah's recipe, made with love and proper ingredients," Agnes said firmly. "Nothing more needed."

The fact that people were lining up to buy more non-magical pastries felt like its own kind of miracle.

By noon, they'd taken reservations for the next two months, sold out of treats that had somehow multiplied to feed everyone who wanted a taste, and attracted a crowd that included visitors from three neighboring towns who'd heard about the "amazing sand globe show."

Ella stood in the middle of the cheerful chaos, feeling simultaneously proud and panicked. This wasn't how businesses were supposed to operate. You couldn't build a sustainable hospitality model on magical brochures and treats that tasted like childhood memories.

Could you?

"Quite a turnout," a familiar voice said behind her.

She turned to find Liam emerging from the hardware store's display. Hands in his jeans pockets he stepped past the festival throng with the easy familiarity of someone who belonged here.

"Your family booth is lovely," she said, grasping for normalcy in the midst of magical chaos. "Katie and your mother are wonderful."

"They like you," he said. "Mom's already planning your adoption into the family, and Katie's composing wedding invitations in her head."

Heat flooded Ella's cheeks. "I'm sure they're just being polite—"

"Ella." His voice was gentle but firm. "In a town this size, people don't waste energy on politeness. If they didn't approve of you, you'd know."

Before she could respond, excited shouts from the sand globe crowd drew their attention. The globe was putting on its most elaborate show yet.

"Brilliant, to bring the sand globe down here." Liam watched over her shoulder as the sand swirled from a lighthouse to a dune to a deep, still lake.

"Is it always crazy like this?" she asked, watching a young couple hold hands as they gazed into the swirling patterns.

Liam's chuckle was warm and reassuring. "You know what's funny? Nobody's asking for explanations. They're just enjoying the experience."

She looked around the crowd, really looked. People weren't demanding rational explanations for the impossible things they were witnessing. They were just enjoying themselves. Calling their friends over. Taking selfies.

"Sarah used to say," Mrs. Frankl appeared beside them, carrying another paper mug of something that smelled like liquid comfort, "that people come to small towns because they want to believe in something larger than themselves. Magic just makes it easier."

"But the business side—"

"Is booming," Mrs. Frankl finished firmly. "We've taken more reservations today than in the past month. People are already asking about returning for Christmas, Easter, summer weddings. The inn hasn't been this popular in years."

As if summoned by their conversation, Agnes appeared with the reservation tablet, her stern face softened by unmistakable satisfaction.

"Christmas, New Year's, fully booked," she

announced. "And a waiting list for Valentine's weekend that's three pages long."

Ella stared at the book, hardly believing the evidence of her own eyes. Months of steady bookings, all generated by a single morning of embracing rather than fighting the inn's particular brand of hospitality magic.

"How?" she asked.

"People want what you're offering," Liam said. "Can't you see?"

Around them, the festival continued its joyful chaos. Children ran between booths with sticky fingers and bright smiles. Couples strolled hand in hand, sharing samples. Older folks mixed with young families, creating the kind of community that felt both timeless and precious.

And at the center of it all, the sand globe continued its gentle magic, showing people visions of connection and hope that made them smile and remember why small towns mattered, why community was worth preserving. Why love—in all its forms—was worth celebrating.

As afternoon faded to wide, rose-colored evening, Ella remembered to check her phone.

Markie (10:47 AM): Your LinkedIn still says you're with us. Technically true for 3 more days.

Markie (11:15 AM): That wasn't a joke. HR needs to know your status.

Markie (11:32 AM): Richard saw your preliminary notes. He's salivating. Boutique inn, prime location, distressed seller. Your commission would be mid-six figures.

Ella didn't feel like a distressed seller.

She was the owner, she needed to remember that.

The owner who needed to help pack up the booth and make sure all her guests were settled. Nobody new was coming in tonight, but lord only knew what mischief her inn was up to.

Her inn.

"Mind if I steal her for a minute?" Liam appeared at the booth, having changed from his hardware store polo into a soft flannel that brought out his eyes.

"Steal away," Agnes said before Ella could respond. "We can manage."

"But the booth—"

"Is in capable hands." Cordelia made a shooing motion. "Go."

Liam offered his hand. "Trust me?"

Against her better judgment, against all corporate logic, she did.

He led her away, down the street toward the beach. The end-of-festival sounds faded, replaced by the rhythm of waves and the calling of gulls. The evening sun painted everything gold and copper. The two islands, nicknamed Mama Lynx and Baby Links, shimmered off the coast, getting the first reds of the sunset.

"Better?" he asked as they reached the sand.

"I don't know what I'm doing," she admitted. "Markie wants numbers. The town wants magic. I want..." She trailed off.

"What do you want, Ella?"

The question hung between them like the festival lights strung between the trees. She looked at him. Steady, patient Liam who fixed what was broken and still believed in magic.

"This," she said. "Today. The way Mrs. Henderson smiled. The way the kids' faces lit up at the sand globe. The way you're looking at me right now."

"How am I looking at you?"

"Like you see me. Not the corporate version or the failed granddaughter or the city girl playing at innkeeper. Just... me."

"I've always seen you," he said. "Even when you were seven with pigtails and grass stains, trying to convince me that chipmunks could be trained to deliver mail."

She laughed, the sound carrying across the water. "I'd forgotten about that."

"I hadn't." He tucked a strand of hair behind her ear, the gesture intimate in the fading light. "I never forgot any of it."

Music drifted from the festival—the evening concert. The Bluegrass Three were starting with a slow one. Without asking, Liam drew her closer, one hand finding her waist, the other keeping hold of hers.

They fit perfectly.

"Dancing on the beach is pretty romantic for a skeptic," she murmured against his shoulder.

"Former skeptic," he corrected. "The inn's been working on me too."

They swayed together as the sun set over Lake Michigan, warm together against the chill of evening. Ella let herself believe, just for this moment, that she could have this. The inn, the town, the man who smelled like fresh pine, sweet cider and home.

Chapter Ten

Monday morning at 11 AM, Ella sat in the innkeeper's turret room, her laptop open on the elegant roll-top desk, cursor blinking accusingly in a document titled "Property Assessment: Starlight Arbor Inn."

Outside the curved windows, Lake Michigan stretched gray and restless under an overcast sky that matched her mood. The weekend's festival magic felt like a distant dream, replaced by the harsh fluorescent reality of corporate expectations.

Focus, she told herself, fingers poised over the keyboard. Professional assessment. Market analysis. Comparable properties. Revenue projections.

She'd been staring at the blank document for twenty

minutes. There was no more coffee in her cup to sip and pretend to think.

Every time she tried to type something factual—square footage, room count, maintenance requirements—the weekend's impossibilities crowded in. How did you put "dancing sand globe" in a property report? What was the market value of teapots that sang in harmony or doors that opened only when the right people stood before them?

The cursor blinked. Waited. Judged.

Finally, she typed: "This property defies conventional valuation methods..."

Then stopped. Because that was absolutely not what Markie Sohn wanted to hear. Or what Pinnacle Hospitality wanted to hear. What her career advancement depended on hearing.

Her phone chirped on the desk beside her laptop. Another email from Markie. She called it up on her laptop.

Subject: Last Chance

Look, I'm going to level with you. Richard wants that property. If you can't close this, I'm sending Bradley up there Tuesday. You know Bradley—he'll have it under contract in 48 hours and take the commission. This is your last chance to prove you're ready for the big leagues. Call me back, or I'll assume you're not interested in your future here.

Ella's stomach dropped. Bradley Patterson—the corporate shark who specialized in "distressed properties." Bradley, who would see the inn's magic as quaint marketing opportunities and the town's charm as exploitable ambiance.

She closed the laptop harder than necessary.

Through the curved windows, the last of the autumn leaves clinging to the maples, bright gold against the gray sky. Soon they'd fall, covering the ground in a carpet that would crunch underfoot and eventually decompose into rich soil for next year's growth. Natural cycles. Things ending to make room for new beginnings.

Was that what she was supposed to do with the inn? Let it end to make room for something new?

Her phone buzzed, Markie's name flashing on the screen. Ella stared at it through four rings, then declined the call.

A commotion out in the lobby interrupted her guilt spiral. Voices in the lobby—one raised, angry, demanding satisfaction. The other lower, soothing, professional.

Mrs. Frankl handling an upset guest.

Ella hurried out to the lobby, pulling on her professional demeanor like armor. Whatever crisis was erupting, she could handle it. That's what she did—solved problems, managed conflicts, turned chaos into order.

She found Mrs. Frankl at the tall, dark-oak front

desk, facing off against a woman in her fifties whose elegant black suit and rigid posture screamed expensive divorce attorney.

"Completely unacceptable," the woman was saying, her voice carrying the particular authority of someone used to getting her way through sheer force of outrage. "I specifically requested the Dune Walker's Room. My husband specifically requested the Harbor Master's Room. Yet somehow—" She waved her phone, which must have the reservation on the screen. "—we've both been assigned to the Rose Suite. Together. As if we're some sort of happy couple instead of two people who can barely stand to be in the same state, let alone the same room."

Mrs. Frankl's expression was a masterpiece of diplomatic neutrality. "Mrs. Weatherby, I understand your frustration. Sometimes our reservation system experiences technical difficulties—"

"Technical difficulties?" Mrs. Weatherby's voice climbed an octave. "Technical difficulties don't move my luggage from one room to another!"

Ella approached the desk, her corporate training kicking in automatically. Upset client. Clear problem. Measurable solution.

"I'm Ella Thompson, the inn's owner," she said, extending her hand with professional warmth. "I'm so sorry you're having difficulties. Let me see what I can do to resolve this."

Mrs. Weatherby turned her ire toward Ella, and for a moment, Ella felt the full force of a woman whose life had imploded and who needed someone to blame. Her hair and makeup were perfect, but her eyes were rimmed red with exhaustion.

"Resolve it?" Mrs. Weatherby laughed bitterly. "Unless you can resolve my entire marriage, I don't think you can help. We're here for Harold's mother's funeral—neutral ground, supposedly. The last thing either of us needs is your establishment trying to play matchmaker."

"Of course not," Ella said smoothly, her fingers already clicking on the computer's keyboard. "Completely understandable. Difficult circumstances. Let me get you sorted immediately."

She pulled up the room assignments, and her heart sank. According to the system, both Weatherbys had indeed been moved to the Rose Suite. Not just assigned—moved. Their original rooms showed as "maintenance required" with notes that definitely hadn't been there last night.

Harbor Master's Room: Plumbing issues, out of service. Dune Walker's Room: Heating system malfunction, unavailable.

Ella knew, with absolute certainty, that both rooms

had been perfectly fine when she'd walked through them this morning, when they had been reserved for early arrivals.

"Let me check our available inventory," she said, buying time while her mind raced. The inn was nearly full for the week—festival bookings, weekend holdovers, the steady autumn business that Mrs. Frankl managed with military precision.

But there—the Blue Room. Still locked, still waiting, but it showed as "available for special circumstances" in the system. When had that changed?

"I can offer you the Blue Room," Ella said carefully. "It's a premium suite, normally reserved for extended stays, but given the circumstances—"

"What about him?" Mrs. Weatherby demanded. "Please tell me you're not expecting me to coordinate with Harold about room assignments. I've spent the last six months coordinating with Harold through lawyers, and I'm frankly done with coordination."

Before Ella could answer, heavy footsteps on the porch announced the arrival of Mr. Weatherby. He was a large man with the kind of presence that filled a room, dressed in an expensive suit that couldn't quite hide his obvious weariness. When he spotted his apparently soon to be ex-wife at the front desk, his face took on the dread of someone facing a familiar battle.

"Margaret," he said with forced politeness. "Having difficulties?"

"The room situation is completely unacceptable," Mrs. Weatherby replied without looking at him. "Apparently their computer system has decided we should be roommates."

"I'll sleep in a tent before I share a room with you," Mr. Weatherby said flatly.

The words hung in the air like a slap. Even Mrs. Frankl winced slightly.

Ella felt the inn's attention focus on the scene with the intensity of a spotlight. The air grew thick, charged with the particular energy that preceded magical intervention. The sand in the sand globe began to fizz.

No, she thought desperately. Not now. Not with these two.

Because looking at the Weatherbys—really looking at them—she could see that they were too far gone. Too entrenched in their anger, too committed to their mutual destruction to be open to whatever healing the inn might offer. The Rose Suite could arrange all the romantic coincidences it wanted; these two had chosen to see each other as enemies rather than wounded people who'd once loved each other enough to marry.

Some things couldn't be fixed. Some people couldn't be saved from themselves.

"Mr. Weatherby," Ella said quickly, "I can arrange

for you to stay at the Harbor Inn downtown. It's a lovely property, very quiet—"

"Absolutely not." His voice was firm. "I'm not being driven away from Sarah Porter's inn because Margaret can't handle being in the same building. This place meant something to my mother. I'm staying."

Mrs. Weatherby's jaw tightened. She pivoted to glare at him. "How dare you—"

"I have a solution," Ella interrupted before the conversation could escalate further. Thank heavens for a flexible mindset. "Mrs. Weatherby, I'll comp your entire stay and provide a voucher for a future visit—when you're ready to enjoy the inn's hospitality on your own terms. Mr. Weatherby, you'll have the Harbor Master's Room once our maintenance team finishes their work this afternoon."

Both Weatherbys stared at her.

"You're refunding her money?" Mr. Weatherby asked.

"I'm providing excellent customer service during a difficult time," Ella replied smoothly. "Sometimes the best solution is the one that gives everyone what they actually need, rather than what they think they want."

Mrs. Weatherby's expression shifted from outrage to surprise to something that might have been gratitude. "That's... actually very reasonable."

"Your mother would have done the same thing," Ella

told Mr. Weatherby gently. "Sarah always said this place should be a refuge, not another source of stress."

He nodded slowly, some of the tension leaving his shoulders. "She would have. Thank you."

As Mrs. Frankl processed the refund and Mrs. Weatherby gathered her things, Ella felt the inn's energy shift. The charged atmosphere eased, the sand globe went quiet. Whatever magical intervention had been building dissipated like steam from a kettle removed from heat.

Sometimes the kindest magic was knowing when not to interfere.

Her phone rang again. Markie, persistent as a tele-marketer.

Ella declined the call.

Then it rang again immediately.

"Excuse me," she told the Weatherbys, stepping away from the desk, toward the tea room. This time she answered.

"Markie, I'm with guests right now—"

"I can see you declining my calls, Thompson." Markie's voice was sharp with impatience. "Very professional. Look, I need those preliminary numbers by end of business today, or I'm sending Bradley up there tomorrow morning."

Through the phone, Ella could hear the familiar sounds of the Chicago office—keyboards clacking, phones ringing, the low hum of aggressive productivity that had once felt like home.

"I'm working on the assessment—"

"Working on it? How hard is it to measure some rooms and count bathrooms?" Markie's tone suggested she was multitasking, probably reviewing other properties while she talked. "Richard from Pinnacle wants to move fast. They're talking about a February closing, complete renovation by summer. This could be a two-million-dollar project, Ella. Your commission alone would be six figures."

Six figures. Ella's stomach twisted as she did the math. More money than she'd ever made in a single transaction. Enough to secure her promotion, her future, her place in the corporate hierarchy she'd spent six years climbing.

"I understand the financial implications—"

"Do you? Because from where I'm sitting, it looks like you're dragging your feet on the opportunity of a lifetime." Markie's voice carried that particular edge that meant her minuscule reserve of patience was empty. "What's going on up there? Are you getting sentimental about some old building?"

Ella glanced around the lobby—at the beautiful antique desk, at Mrs. Frankl efficiently handling the Weatherby situation, at the way the morning light fell through the tall windows and painted everything in shades of gold and possibility.

"It's complicated," she said finally.

"Either the property makes financial sense or it doesn't. Either you're ready for senior-level responsibility or you're not." Markie's sigh was audible. "Look, I like you. You're smart, you're competent, you usually deliver. But sentiment doesn't pay the bills. Send me those numbers by five, or I'm pulling you off this project and sending someone who can handle it."

The line went dead.

Ella stared at her phone. Five o'clock. Six hours to reduce the Starlight Arbor Inn to a series of data points that would justify its transformation into another cookie-cutter boutique property.

"Everything all right?" Mrs. Frankl's voice was carefully neutral, but her sharp eyes missed nothing.

"Just work," Ella said, forcing a smile. "Chicago checking in."

"Mmm." Mrs. Frankl's expression suggested she knew exactly what kind of "checking in" that had been. "The Weatherbys are settled. He's in the Harbor Master's Room, she's checked out and on her way to the Harbor Inn. I called Melanie, so she's expecting her."

"Good. That's good." Ella pocketed her phone, trying to push away the image of Bradley Patterson arriving tomorrow with his measuring tape and his profit projections. "I should get back to—"

"Rose Suite acting up again?"

The familiar voice made her heart skip. Liam stood in the doorway, tool belt around his waist and an expression that suggested he'd heard enough of her phone conversation to understand she was dealing with more than plumbing problems.

"Just a reservation mix-up," she said, grateful for the excuse to focus on something fixable. "Though the room did seem... enthusiastic about its matchmaking attempts."

"Enthusiastic." Liam's smile was warm and knowing. "That's one word for it."

They fell into step together, heading for the stairs. Being near him always made her feel more centered, more like herself instead of the corporate persona she wore like armor.

"Bad phone call?" he asked as they climbed.

"Work. They want numbers. Data. A professional assessment that makes sense on paper." She gestured helplessly. "How do you quantify magic?"

"You don't," he said simply.

They reached the second floor, and Liam led her to the Rose Suite's door. It stood slightly ajar, as if teasing them. Mr. Weatherby's suitcases sat just outside the door, in the hall.

The room was pristine, as always, but something felt different. The air held a subtle charge, like the aftermath of a storm. The wallpaper's rose pattern seemed more vivid than usual, and the scent of actual roses filled the space despite the October date.

"It's trying really hard," Ella observed, stepping inside.

"Some people are more receptive than others." Liam knelt beside the ornate radiator, though they both knew it was working perfectly. "Your couple just weren't ready for what this room offers."

"Which is?"

"Second chances. New beginnings. The possibility that love can survive even when everything else falls apart." He looked up at her, his deep-ocean blue eyes serious. "But you have to be open to it. You have to choose it."

The words hung between them, heavy with meaning that went beyond room dynamics and magical interference.

"Liam," she started, then stopped. Because what could she say? That she was falling for him but might be gone by the end of the week? That every moment they spent together made it harder to imagine leaving, but leaving might be the only way to save her career?

He stood, brushing dust from his knees that definitely hadn't been there. "The radiator's fine. Just needed some attention."

"Like most things around here."

"Yeah." His voice was soft, intimate in the rose-scented air. "Like most things."

They stood in the doorway, neither quite willing to break the moment. Ella was acutely aware of his nearness, the way his soft chamois shirt brought out the blue of his eyes, how his presence made her feel simultaneously safe and reckless.

"I should ask," she said, grasping for normalcy. "How do you know so much about what the rooms do? Their... personalities?"

Liam's smile turned rueful. "Katie used to say the Rose Suite was like couple's therapy with wallpaper. She wasn't wrong." He paused, then added quietly, "My ex-girlfriend, Amanda—she always said I was married to this town before I could be married to her. Said I'd never leave, never grow, never want anything bigger than Green Arbor could offer."

"And?"

"Maybe she was right about the first part. I don't want to leave." His gaze found hers. "But maybe she was wrong about what marriage means. Maybe it's not about finding someone who makes you want to escape your life. Maybe it's about finding someone who makes you want to build a better life right where you are."

The air in the Rose Suite went still. Ella felt her pulse quicken, felt the dangerous pull of possibility and promise and everything she'd convinced herself she couldn't have.

"Liam—"

Her phone buzzed against her hip. Text message.

Last chance: Brad's flying out Tuesday if I don't hear from you.

Reality crashed back like cold water. The corporate world, waiting. Her career, hanging in the balance. The assessment that was due in five hours and contained exactly one sentence.

"I should get back to work," she said, the words tasting like ash.

"Right." Liam stepped back, creating professional distance though his eyes held disappointment."

"Thank you For coming. For... understanding."

He paused at the threshold. "Ella? For what it's worth, I think Amanda was wrong about a lot of things. Including what you're capable of choosing."

After he left, Ella stood alone in the Rose Suite, surrounded by the scent of impossible roses and the weight of impossible choices. Through the windows, the lake stretched gray and endless toward a horizon that might hold Chicago, might hold her future, might hold everything she was supposed to want.

Her phone chimed again. Another email, another

demand, another reminder that the real world was waiting for her to stop playing innkeeper and return to being the ambitious corporate raptor who knew the price of everything and the value of nothing.

She pulled up the assessment document on her phone, stared at the single pathetic sentence she'd managed to write.

This property defies conventional valuation methods...

The cursor blinked. Waited. Judged.

Outside, clouds were gathering over the lake, promising the kind of autumn storm that would remind everyone that winter was coming, that seasons changed whether you were ready or not.

Ella clicked the phone screen off.

The inn settled around her with a sound like a sigh.

Chapter Eleven

The first thing Liam noticed as he pulled into the inn's gravel drive that evening was the restless energy crackling through the air—and not just from the storm building over Lake Michigan.

Ella's battered Focus sat even more askew in its parking spot, as if she'd abandoned it in haste rather than parked it with intention. Through the kitchen windows, he could see movement—quick, agitated, the kind of frantic activity that spoke of nervous energy with nowhere productive to go.

The lake stretched before him, its usual late-afternoon calm replaced by choppy whitecaps that caught the last rays of sunlight like scattered coins. To the west, a wall of dark clouds was building with unseasonable intensity, the kind of October storm that came fast and hit hard. The air pressure had that particular weight to it that made his old shoulder injury ache.

The forecast hadn't said anything about storms, but by four o'clock, the text warnings were coming from the local weather center: Batten down. He'd done the two B-and-B's down the hills and the post office. Katie had already done the hardware store, and dad had handled the rambling family house and the elementary school.

Liam hefted his toolbox from the truck bed. The inn's windows were secure, the gutters clear, the heating system serviced and ready for whatever autumn could throw at it. But the storm gave him an excuse to check that the storm shutters were secure. And check on Ella, to make sure she was weathering whatever corporate pressure had followed.

Maybe tie down that Focus.

The memory of yesterday's conversation in the Rose Suite had been replaying in his mind all day—the way she'd looked when her phone had pinged with another demand from Chicago, the defeated slope of her shoulders when she'd pulled away from him. He'd spent seventeen years watching people leave Green Arbor for bigger opportunities. The thought that Ella might be next made his chest tight with a familiar dread.

The front door stood open despite the dropping temperature, unusual for Mrs. Frankl, who believed in proper climate control and energy efficiency. As he climbed the porch steps, he could hear voices from inside—the housekeeping sisters, by the sound of it, their familiar chatter mixing with the distant clatter of dishes.

"—told her she needed to eat something," Cordelia was saying as he entered the lobby. "But she just keeps moving things around like she's trying to organize the whole world into making sense."

"The girl's in a state," Agnes agreed grimly. "Haven't seen anyone that wound up since that corporate fellow tried to buy the place five years back."

"Where is she?" Liam asked, setting his toolbox by the door.

"Kitchen," Beatrice replied, emerging from the dining room with an armload of table linens. "Though she's been in every room today, rearranging furniture that didn't need rearranging and polishing things that were already clean."

Liam found Ella exactly as described—in constant motion, wiping down counters that gleamed, reorganizing spice jars that were already perfectly arranged. She'd pulled her hair back in a messy bun that suggested she'd been trying not to run her hands through it and failing. Sarah's gray cardigan hung loose on her frame.

She looked like someone trying to outrun her own thoughts.

"Evening," he said from the doorway.

She spun around, startled. Her face carried the shadows that came from sleepless nights and impossible decisions.

"Liam." She attempted a smile that didn't quite reach her eyes. "I wasn't expecting—is something wrong?"

"Storm coming in. Thought I'd check the shutters, make sure everything's battened down." He gestured toward the gathering darkness outside. "Forecast says it could be a rough one."

"Of course. Windows. Very responsible." She turned back to the already-spotless counter, scrubbing with unnecessary vigor. "I'm sure everything's fine, but it's good to check. Always good to check things that might need checking."

She was babbling, which meant she was rattled. Liam stepped into the kitchen, noting the subtle signs of stress that probably weren't visible to anyone who didn't know her well. The way she held her shoulders too tight. The particular rhythm of her movements, too fast and too precise. The fact that she hadn't eaten—Cordelia had mentioned it, and the untouched sandwich on the counter confirmed it.

"How about I start with the third floor?" he said, giving her space to compose herself. "Work my way down?"

"Perfect. Yes. Third floor first, then second, then…" She gestured vaguely. "Systematic approach. Very logical."

Through the kitchen windows, the first fat raindrops began hitting the glass, driven sideways by wind that was picking up speed. The temperature had dropped ten degrees since he'd arrived, and the air had that electric quality that preceded serious weather.

Liam made his way through the inn, testing window latches that didn't need testing, checking radiators that hummed along perfectly. But he couldn't help noticing the signs of Ella's restless day everywhere—furniture moved slightly from its usual positions, books rearranged, even the guest bathroom towels refolded into different patterns.

The inn itself felt charged, responsive to her emotional state in that way he'd learned to recognize over the years. Doors opened more easily than usual, as if trying to speed her passage. The floorboards' usual musical creaks were softer, more soothing. Even the air seemed to carry a faint scent of lavender—the inn's equivalent of offering a cup of calming tea.

By the time he'd worked his way back to the main floor, the storm had arrived in earnest. Rain hammered against the windows in sheets, and wind howled around the corners of the building with the particular fury of lake-effect weather. The temperature was dropping fast enough that he could see his breath when he stepped near the windows.

"Quite a blow," Mrs. Frankl observed, appearing in the lobby with her arms full of pillar candles and battery-powered lanterns. "Power might flicker. Best to be prepared."

"Need help with anything?"

"Agnes and the girls are handling the guest floors. Arthur Pemberton's in the Stargazer Suite—lovely gentleman, here for his late wife's birthday. They used to come every year." She set the emergency supplies on the front desk with practiced efficiency. "Harold Weatherby's in the Harbor Master's Room. Poor man's barely spoken since his wife left yesterday."

"And Ella?"

Mrs. Frankl's expression softened slightly. "Still in the kitchen, I believe. Making enough tea to float a ship, though she hasn't drunk a drop of it."

The lights flickered. Once, twice, then went out entirely.

The inn plunged into darkness—but not complete darkness. Almost immediately, a warm golden glow began emanating from the walls themselves, the same impossible light he'd witnessed the morning Ella had arrived. It was subtle, barely brighter than candlelight, but somehow it filled every corner and banished the oppressive blackness that should have followed the power failure.

"Well," Mrs. Frankl said calmly, as if glowing walls were perfectly normal. "That's convenient."

From the kitchen came the sound of something metallic hitting the floor, followed by Ella's frustrated voice: "Perfect. Just perfect."

Liam found her standing in the middle of the kitchen, surrounded by scattered tea strainers, staring at the golden light that painted everything in warm honey tones. She looked like a painting herself—wild curls escaping her bun, cardigan slipping off one shoulder, eyes wide with wonder and exasperation.

"Emergency generator?" she asked hopefully.

"Doesn't glow gold," he said gently. "You know what this is."

"I know what it looks like. I don't know what it is." She bent to gather the scattered strainers, her movements jerky. "I don't know anything anymore. I can't write a simple property assessment. I can't return my boss's calls. I can't even make tea without dropping half the pieces"

"Hey." Liam crossed to her, crouching to help collect a wayward spoon. "When's the last time you ate something?"

"I'm not hungry."

"That's not what I asked."

She paused in her gathering, considering. "Sunday? Maybe? I had that apple at the festival, and some of Cordelia's cookies..."

"Ella." He stood, hands full of rescued tea equipment. "It's Tuesday."

"I know what day it is." But color flooded her cheeks, and he could see her making the calculation. "I've been busy. Stressed. Food seems... complicated."

Before he could respond, voices drifted in from the lobby—the housekeeping sisters, cheerful despite the power outage, and two male voices he didn't immediately recognize. The guests, probably drawn from their rooms by the storm and the sudden darkness.

"We should check on everyone," Ella said, straightening her cardigan with shaking hands. "Make sure they're comfortable, have what they need. Professional hospitality standards."

"Mrs. Frankl's got it handled," Liam said. "She's been managing storms here longer than either of us has been alive."

But Ella was already moving toward the lobby. Liam followed, noting how the inn's golden glow seemed to pulse gently, responding to the number of people it was sheltering.

The lobby had transformed into something from a fairy tale. The impossible light turned everything soft and dreamlike—the sand globe on its pedestal, swirling with lazy contentment, the wide mahogany staircase with its carved banister, the tall windows that framed the storm's fury outside. But no one was here.

Everyone had gravitated toward the front parlor's warmth, drawn by some instinct for community that storms awakened in even the most solitary souls.

And the roaring fireplace.

Liam had passed through the parlor countless times over the years, but tonight the room revealed itself as something special. It occupied the front corner of the inn, positioned to catch both morning and afternoon light through tall windows that even when shuttered and protected by the porch framed the storm's dramatic display. The walls were painted in a warm sky blue with subtle gold undertones that seemed to glow from within, creating an atmosphere that was both elegant and welcoming.

Two matching sofas upholstered in deep burgundy velvet faced each other across a low green-tinted glass table held up by a big gray-white chunk of driftwood. The wood's grain flowed in natural curves that suggested water or win. Between them sat armchairs in complementary patterns—one in sage green with tiny gold flowers, another in cream with burgundy stripes that picked up the sofas' color.

The focal point of the room was the fireplace, a masterpiece of local stone that rose from floor to ceiling.

The stones varied in color from deep gray to warm honey, all worn smooth by decades of Lake Michigan's waves before finding their way into this room. The mantelpiece was carved from another piece of driftwood, its surface populated with framed photographs, shells and Petoskey stones, and a brass clock whose gentle tick offered a steady counterpoint to the storm's chaotic percussion.

The fire cast dancing shadows across the inner walls, lined with built-in bookcases. The shelves held an eclectic mix—leather-bound classics next to paperback mysteries, local histories sharing space with volumes of poetry, their spines creating a warm tapestry of colors and textures. Small reading lamps with green glass shades were positioned throughout the room, though they remained dark, the inn's magical glow providing all the illumination needed.

The hardwood floors gleamed with decades of careful maintenance, partially covered by an enormous Persian rug in deep blues and golds that tied the room's color palette together. Its pattern was complex enough to reward close examination but subtle enough never to overwhelm, worn soft in the paths where generations of guests had walked.

Mrs. Frankl moved through the space with quiet efficiency, lighting real candles despite the inn's other-worldly illumination. The additional light created layers of warmth, filling corners and casting a gentle glow across faces. She'd arranged the emergency supplies on a side table—more battery-powered lanterns, a stack of extra blankets, and a tray of sweets and savories, with teacups and an insulated pot that smelled of her special storm-weather cocoa.

Agnes, Beatrice, and Cordelia had claimed the burgundy sofa closest to the fire, Agnes in the center with her sisters flanking her like a matched set of book-ends. They wore their best housedresses despite being caught at work by the storm, and each held a teacup from the inn's collection of mismatched china. Agnes's cup was painted with tiny roses, Beatrice's featured a hunting scene, and Cordelia's displayed cheerful yellow daisies—perfectly suited to their personalities.

"Quite a storm," Agnes was saying to the room in general. "Haven't seen one this fierce in October since '98."

"The inn likes storms," Cordelia added comfortably. "Always has. Something about the drama, the way they bring people together."

In the sage green armchair sat a man Liam didn't recognize—older, well-dressed despite his obvious grief, with silver white hair and kind eyes behind wire-rimmed glasses. He held his teacup with the careful attention of someone using ritual to manage emotion.

"Arthur Pemberton," the man introduced himself as

Liam and Ella entered. "I'm sorry for the circumstances, but this is quite lovely. Eleanor always said storms made this place feel most like home."

"Eleanor was your wife?" Ella asked gently, settling onto the edge of the remaining sofa, close to Arthur, with the particular care of someone managing both physical and emotional exhaustion.

"Forty-three years together," Arthur said, his voice soft with memory. "We came here every October for our anniversary. She passed last spring, but I couldn't bear to miss this year. Felt like she'd be disappointed if I didn't show up."

From the window seat closest to the storm came another voice, thick with its own grief: "My mother felt the same way about this place."

Harold Weatherby emerged from the shadows, a large man made smaller by loss. He'd changed out of his suit and into jeans and a University of Michigan sweatshirt, He moved carefully, as if his bones hurt, and settled into the cream-striped armchair with visible relief.

"Harold Weatherby," he said by way of introduction. "My mother, Evelyn, passed last week. I'm here for the funeral tomorrow." He paused, looking around the room. "She met my father here during the blizzard of '52. Always said this parlor was where she learned what love could weather."

The room seemed to pulse gently at his words, the golden light growing slightly warmer. Outside, the storm continued its assault, but inside the parlor felt like the safest place in the world—a refuge that had sheltered conversations like this for over a century.

Liam let himself settle on the burgundy sofa next to Ella, close enough to feel the warmth radiating from her body but maintaining the careful distance of someone aware they were in public. The cushions were perfectly broken in, supportive but soft, upholstered in velvet that had just started to wear to silk in places where countless people had found comfort.

"This room has heard a lot of stories," Mrs. Frankl said, settling into a straight-backed chair she'd pulled from the writing desk in the corner. Even in crisis, she maintained perfect posture.

"Would you like to hear another one?" Liam found himself asking, the words emerging before he'd consciously decided to speak. Must be all the dreaming lately; he seemed full of stories.

All eyes turned to him expectantly. The fire crackled in the hearth, sending sparks up the chimney and casting shifting patterns of light and shadow across the assembled faces. The storm's howling provided a dramatic soundtrack, punctuated by thunder that rattled the windows in their frames.

"My grandfather used to tell me stories about this

place," he continued, his voice taking on the rhythm of someone settling into a tale. "About the magic that lived here, about why storms seemed to bring out the inn's true nature."

"Magic?" Arthur asked, but his tone suggested curiosity rather than skepticism.

"The legend of the whispering lynx," Liam said, and felt the room's attention focus like a spotlight. "My grandfather swore it was true, said his own grandfather had seen it happen."

He could feel Ella's gaze on his profile, warm and intent. The last time he'd told this story, it had been to a festival crowd, entertaining rather than believing. Tonight felt different—intimate, sacred, like sharing something precious with people who would understand its value.

"They say, long ago, a lynx roamed these dunes," he began, his voice finding the cadence his grandfather had used, the rhythm that made stories feel true rather than merely told. "Beautiful creature, golden eyes like captured starlight, fur the color of winter moonlight on snow. paws like giant mittens!" He spread his fingers wide.

"But this wasn't just any lynx—it could see into people's hearts, could sense love and longing and the connections that bound souls together."

The wind picked up outside, howling around the

inn's corners with renewed fury. Inside, everyone leaned forward slightly, drawn into the story's spell.

"The lynx became a guardian of sorts, watching over the land, protecting those who came seeking something they'd lost or something they'd never found. When travelers appeared—lost, heartsick, alone—the lynx would whisper to them on the wind, guiding them toward healing, toward each other, toward home."

"One winter, a terrible fire swept across the land," Liam continued, his voice growing softer so everyone had to listen carefully over the storm. "The flames threatened everything—the forest, the animals, the people who lived here. The lynx saw the destruction coming and made a choice. It ran into the heart of the fire, calling to the wind spirits for help, offering its own life to save the land it loved."

Thunder crashed overhead, so perfectly timed it seemed part of the story. The three sisters jumped, then smiled at their own reactions.

"The wind spirits heard the lynx's sacrifice and were moved by such love," Liam said. "They froze the fire where it stood, transforming the flames into golden sand dunes and the lynx's tears into the lake itself. But the lynx's spirit didn't die—it became part of the land, part of the wind, part of the magic that draws people here when they need healing most."

"They say," he finished, his voice dropping to barely

above a whisper, "that if you see the lynx during a storm, it means love is about to find you. Or that you're about to find your way home."

The parlor fell silent except for the fire's gentle crackling and the storm's distant fury.

"Eleanor would have loved that story," Arthur said finally, his voice thick with emotion. "She always insisted this place was magical. Said it felt like being held by something larger than herself."

"My mother told a similar story," Harold added quietly. "About meeting my father here during that blizzard. Said she was lost in more ways than one when she arrived, but the storm forced her to stay, forced her to meet the man who became her anchor."

Agnes, Beatrice, and Cordelia exchanged one of their telepathic looks.

"Sarah used to say," Agnes began, "that storms brought out the inn's true nature."

"Like it knew people needed gathering," Beatrice continued.

"Needed reminding that they weren't alone," Cordelia finished.

"And it certainly explains all those T-shirts with the oversized paws running all across them," Mr. Weatherby.

"And the plushies," said Cordelia. "What?" She looked at Agnes. "I only have half a dozen."

"That we know of," Beatrice said.

Ella laughed softly. Beside him on the velvet sofa, her presence warm and distracting. She'd drawn her feet up under her, Sarah's cardigan wrapped around her like armor, but he saw the tension in her shoulders, the way she held herself carefully as if afraid she might break.

When thunder crashed particularly loud, she instinctively moved closer to him. Just an inch or two, barely noticeable to anyone watching, but he felt the shift like an electric current. The scent of her hair—vanilla and something floral—mixed with the parlor's atmosphere of wood smoke and beeswax candles.

"Not scared of storms, are you, Thompson?" he asked quietly, pitched for her ears alone.

Her smile was rueful, tired around the edges. "Only of what comes after them."

He understood immediately. Clear skies meant normalcy returning, meant no excuse for this closeness, meant she'd have to face whatever corporate storm was building in Chicago.

Outside, the storm was reaching its peak. Rain hammered in waves, and wind howled through the eaves with enough force to make the whole building creak and sigh. Weather service said less than an hour, total, but enough rain for the whole month.

But inside the parlor, the conversations had grown quieter, more intimate, as people shared the kind of stories that only emerged in the safety of unexpected sanctuary. Arthur described his and Eleanor's last visit to the inn, how she'd insisted on walking to the lighthouse despite her failing health, how she'd stood on the shore and whispered something to the wind that he'd never been able to hear.

Harold Weatherby shared memories of his mother, and Agnes gave him one of her own memories: How Evelyn had always brought them gifts from her travels, how she'd loved hearing about the inn's daily dramas and small triumphs.

Liam watched Ella's profile in the firelight, noting the way exhaustion had softened her usual corporate sharpness, made her look younger and more vulnerable. Her phone sat silent; he'd noticed her turn it face down on the coffee table when she'd sat down, the first time he'd seen her voluntarily disconnect from Chicago's demands.

"Quite a crowd for a Monday in October," he observed quietly.

"Mrs. Frankl says storms call people who need calling," Ella replied, her voice thoughtful. "Arthur came for Eleanor's birthday. Harold for his mother's funeral. The sisters stayed late because of the weather warning." She paused, looking around the room.

"What about you?" The question slipped out. "What called you here tonight?"

She was quiet for so long he thought she might not

answer. Outside, the storm seemed to be settling into a steadier rhythm, less violent but no less persistent.

"Fear," she said finally. "The kind that keeps you moving so you don't have to think. I missed Markie's deadline today. Haven't returned her calls. I can't seem to write a simple property assessment because every time I try, all I can think about is how wrong it would be to reduce this place to square footage and revenue projections."

Liam felt something cold settle in his stomach. "What happens when you miss deadlines?"

"In my world? Someone else gets sent to do your job." Her laugh was hollow. "Someone named Bradley Patterson, who specializes in 'distressed properties' and has never met a historic building he couldn't turn into a profitable chain hotel."

"When?"

"Tomorrow, probably. Maybe Thursday if I'm lucky." She pulled the cardigan tighter around herself. "Bradley doesn't believe in magic or sentiment or anything that can't be quantified in a quarterly report. He'll see this place as prime lakefront real estate with good bones and potential to expand."

The thought of someone like that getting his hands on the inn, treating it like just another acquisition to be stripped and commodified, made Liam see red. This place was more than a building—it was a sanctuary, a keeper of stories, a living piece of the community's heart.

"What would happen if you just said no?" he asked. "Told them you're not selling?"

"Then my career ends and I'm unemployed in a town where I own an inn that has a mountain of fixed costs and that I have no idea how to run." Her voice cracked slightly. "I've spent six years building my reputation in commercial real estate. It's all I know how to do, all I'm qualified for. If I burn that bridge…"

"You'd have to trust that something else would catch you," he finished quietly.

"Exactly. And I've never been good at that kind of trust."

They sat in silence for a moment, watching the fire paint shifting shadows across the patterns in the carpets.

"You know," Liam said carefully, "my grandfather used to say the inn had a way of calling people when they were ready for change. Not when they thought they were ready, but when they actually were."

"And you think that's what's happening here?"

"I think you haven't been able to write that assessment for however many days because some part of you knows it would be wrong." He turned to face her more fully. Firelight brought out the gold flecks in her eyes. "I think you're fighting a battle between who you've trained yourself to be and who you actually are."

"That's a pretty theory," she said softly. "But theories don't pay bills or build careers or—"

Thunder crashed overhead, so loud and sudden that everyone in the parlor jumped. For a moment, the inn's golden glow flickered, dimmed, then surged back brighter than before.

"Did anyone else feel that?" Arthur asked, looking around with wonder.

"Like the building shifted?" Harold added. "But not in a bad way. More like... settling into itself?"

Mrs. Frankl smiled knowingly. "The inn does that sometimes. Usually when it approves of a conversation."

Ella stared at her. "The inn approves of conversations?"

"Among other things," Agnes said with a satisfied nod.

"It has opinions," Beatrice added.

"Strong ones," Cordelia finished.

Arthur looked at Harold Weatherby. "Right," he said, sounding unconvinced.

Outside, the storm was beginning to ease. The wind had lost some of its fury, and the rain had settled into a steadier, gentler rhythm. But nobody seemed in any hurry to leave the parlor's warmth and safety.

Liam found himself studying Ella's hands where they rested on the sofa's arm—small, competent hands that bore no calluses from physical work but showed the care she took in everything she touched. City hands that were learning to tend magical things.

"Can I ask you something?" he said quietly.

"Of course."

"If money weren't a factor—if you had enough to live on, enough to feel secure—what would you choose?"

She was quiet for a long time, staring into the fire. When she finally spoke, her voice was barely above a whisper.

"This. I'd choose this. The inn, the town, the way people's faces light up when something impossible happens and they decide to believe in it anyway." She turned to look at him, a glint of tears in her eyes. "I'd choose afternoon tea with Mrs. Frankl, and cooking lessons with the sisters, and guests who find exactly what they need even when they don't know what that is."

"And?" he prompted gently.

Color rose in her cheeks. "And you. I'd choose you, if you'd let me. If you could forgive me for taking so long to figure out what matters."

The words hung between them like a gift, precious and fragile. Liam felt his heart do something complicated in his chest, a sensation he hadn't experienced since he'd been foolish enough to fall for someone who didn't understand the difference between staying and being trapped.

"Ella," he said, his voice rough.

But before he could continue, the lights flickered back on. Not all at once, but gradually, as if the inn was reluctant to break the spell of candlelight and golden glow. The electric fixtures seemed harsh after the magical illumination, too bright and too ordinary.

Around the parlor, people began to stir—gathering empty teacups, folding blankets, preparing to return to their individual rooms and lives. The communal spell was breaking, the way it always did when ordinary time reasserted itself.

"I should check the guest floors," Ella said, standing with visible reluctance. "Make sure everyone has what they need, that the power's back everywhere."

"I'll help," Liam said, not ready to let the evening end, not ready to lose the connection they'd found in the storm's sanctuary.

They made their way through the inn together, checking that lights were functioning and heat was restored. Each room they entered felt ordinary after the parlor's enchanted atmosphere—functional and comfortable but lacking the magic that had wrapped around them like a shared secret.

By the time they'd finished their rounds, the storm had settled into steady rain and distant thunder. Arthur had retired to the Stargazer Suite with a thermos of Mrs. Frankl's cocoa. Harold had gone to his room to call his daughter with updates about the funeral arrangements. The housekeeping sisters had gathered their things and prepared to head home, satisfied that the inn had weathered another storm without incident.

Mrs. Frankl was banking the parlor fire when Liam and Ella returned to the main floor, her movements efficient and practiced.

"Everything secure?" she asked.

"All clear," Ella confirmed. "Thank you for managing everything so smoothly."

"That's what storms are for," Mrs. Frankl said. "Bringing out the best in people and places."

She gathered her things and headed for the door, pausing only to squeeze Ella's shoulder gently. "The inn knows what it's doing, dear. Trust it."

After she left, Liam and Ella stood alone in the lobby, suddenly awkward with each other now that the storm's intimacy had passed. The sand globe swirled gently on its pedestal, content and peaceful, showing no sign of the evening's drama.

"I should let you get some rest," Liam said, though every instinct screamed at him to stay, to hold onto whatever they'd found in the parlor's warmth.

"Will you be okay?" Ella asked. "The roads might be rough with all this rain."

"I'll be fine. Done this drive in worse weather." He headed for the door, then stopped, something in her expression making him turn back. "Will you be here tomorrow?"

The question carried weight they both understood.

"I don't know," she said. She sighed. "I wish I did, but I don't know."

Liam nodded, accepting the honesty even as it gave a chill to his chest. He'd been here before—caring about someone who was deciding whether staying was worth the risk.

"For what it's worth," he said, hand on the door latch, "I think you're braver than you know."

Chapter Twelve

Tuesday morning arrived gray and subdued, as if the earth itself was recovering from the storm's fury. From the kitchen windows, Lake Michigan stretched out to the horizon, its surface still restless with leftover energy, whitecaps catching the pale morning light.

She'd never been here when the storm was cold. She'd been a Summer Person, in and out in a single season. Hadn't even thought of the people who would stay here year-round.

Could she be one of them, now?

Her phone sat face-down on the kitchen counter, silent now but heavy with accusation. Seven missed texts from Markie. Texts that had progressed from professional urgency to barely contained fury. The last one, received at 6:47 AM, had been admirably direct:

Brad lands at Traverse City at 12:55. Be ready to hand over this project or clean out your desk.

Ella had read it once, then turned the phone over and tried to pretend the corporate world didn't exist. Her hands shook slightly as she attempted to make coffee with the machine that had behaved itself perfectly since that first day—a small mercy she didn't want to examine too closely.

The inn felt different this morning. Quieter, somehow, but not empty. More like a theater after a particularly moving performance, still humming with the energy of something important that had happened within its walls. Last night's storm had done more than clear the air—it had cleared away the last of her pretenses, leaving her with a clarity that was both terrifying and oddly peaceful.

She'd chosen. In the parlor's firelight, surrounded by people who understood loss and healing, she'd finally admitted what her heart had been trying to tell her for days. The inn wasn't just a property to be assessed and sold.

It was home.

It was a calling.

It was the life she wanted to build. If she was brave enough to reach for it.

Fight for it.

"You're up early." Mrs. Frankl's voice came from the doorway, carrying its usual note of calm observation. She wore her navy cardigan buttoned to the throat despite the mild morning, and her silver hair was arranged in its customary perfect bun. But something in her expression suggested today would be different from their usual efficient interactions.

"Couldn't sleep," Ella admitted, abandoning her attempt at breakfast preparation. "Too much to think about."

"Thinking rarely solved anything on an empty stomach." Mrs. Frankl moved into the kitchen with her usual purposeful grace, her dark eyes taking inventory of the untouched breakfast ingredients, the coffee that remained undrunk, the phone that sat like an unexploded bomb on the counter. "When did you last eat a proper meal?"

"I'm not really hungry—"

"Not what I asked." Mrs. Frankl's tone carried the particular authority of someone who'd spent decades caring for people who didn't know how to care for themselves. "You can't make clear decisions on an empty stomach."

Ella found herself studying the older woman's face, noting the lines that spoke of years spent managing other people's crises, the hands that moved with the confidence of someone who'd learned to find order in chaos. "How do you do it? Stay so calm when everything's falling apart?"

"Practice," Mrs. Frankl said. "And perspective. Most crises aren't actually crises. They're just life asking you to choose what matters most." She paused, considering Ella with those sharp dark eyes. "Though I suspect today might be different."

"Bradley Patterson will be here by two o'clock," Ella said, the words tasting like defeat. "Markie's golden boy, the one who specializes in turning historic properties into profitable chains. He'll take measurements, crunch numbers, and have this place under contract by Friday."

"Will he?" Mrs. Frankl's voice held a note of something that might have been amusement. "How interesting."

Before Ella could ask what that meant, voices drifted in from the lobby. Agnes and the rumble of Harold Weatherby, preparing to leave for his mother's funeral. She should check on him, make sure he had everything he needed, offer whatever comfort professional hospitality could provide.

"Go," Mrs. Frankl said gently, handing her half a peanut butter and marmalade sandwich. "Take care of your guests. I'll prepare something for later."

"What kind of something?"

Mrs. Frankl only smiled, and hurried her out toward the lobby.

Harold looked fine in a black suit with white shirt and carrying a small overnight bag. In the morning light, he looked less burdened than he had during the storm.

"Mr. Weatherby," she greeted him. "How are you feeling this morning?"

"Better than I expected," he admitted, setting down his bag to shake her hand. "Last night... being able to talk about her, to share those memories with people who understood—it helped. Thank you for that."

"Absolutely," she said. "It was a gift to hear your memories of her."

"A gift." He looked around the lobby, taking in the sand globe that swirled gently in its morning sunlight, the polished wood and brass that gleamed with decades of careful attention. "Mother always said this place knew how to heal hearts. I never understood what she meant until now."

"I'm so sorry for your loss," Ella said, meaning it more than the professional condolences she'd offered countless times before. "Your mother sounds like she was a remarkable woman."

"She was. And she loved this place." His expression grew serious. "I hope whoever takes care of it next understands what they're inheriting. This isn't just a building—it's a legacy."

The words hit Ella like a gentle slap, reminding her that her choice affected more than just her own future. People like Harold, like Arthur, like countless others who'd found healing within these walls. They were counting on her to preserve something precious.

"I'll do my best to make sure it's protected," she said, though the promise felt fragile against the weight of corporate pressure.

She'd have to work to make it stronger, then.

After Harold left, Ella checked on Arthur, who was extending his stay through the weekend. "Eleanor always loved October here," he explained, sitting in one of the parlor's window seats with a cup of coffee and a contented expression. "I can see why. There's something peaceful about this place, especially after a storm."

"You're welcome to stay as long as you need," Ella told him, and found she meant it completely. This was what innkeeping was supposed to be—providing sanctuary for people who needed time to heal, to remember, to find their way forward.

By the time she returned to the kitchen, Mrs. Frankl had transformed the space. The island had been cleared and set with the same silver tea service Ella remembered from their previous lesson, but today it felt more formal, more ceremonial. Candles flickered despite the morning light, and the air carried the complex scent of herbs and flowers that seemed to promise transformation.

"Sit," Mrs. Frankl commanded gently, gesturing to one of the high stools. "Today's lesson is different from before."

"How different?"

"Today you learn why the tea service matters. Why your grandmother spent sixty years perfecting blends that can't be found in any catalog, why people travel across the country for a simple cup of tea." Mrs. Frankl moved to the far wall, running her fingers along the yellow-painted wainscoting until she found what she was looking for.

A section of the wall swung inward on hidden hinges, revealing a narrow cabinet Ella had never noticed. Inside, illuminated by soft LED lighting, sat dozens of glass jars filled with loose tea blends. Each jar bore a handwritten label in careful script—some in Sarah's familiar handwriting, others in older hands that spoke of generations of innkeepers.

"Oh, my," Ella breathed, sliding off her stool to examine the hidden collection. "How many are there?"

"Forty-seven distinct blends," Mrs. Frankl said, lifting jars with reverent care. "Some go back to your great-grandmother's time. Others your grandmother created herself, based on the specific needs of guests who found their way here."

Ella read the labels aloud, each one a story waiting to be told: "Courage. New Beginnings. Letting Go. Second

Chances." She paused at one jar labeled in Sarah's precise script: "Coming Home."

"That was her last creation," Mrs. Frankl said softly. "Made it the month before she died. Said she was preparing for someone special."

"Someone special?"

"You, dear."

The words washed over Ella like a warm wave, carrying emotions she wasn't prepared to handle. She gripped the edge of the cabinet, staring at the jar that contained her grandmother's final gift—faith that her granddaughter would eventually find her way back to where she belonged.

"I don't understand," she whispered. "How could she know? I didn't even know myself until..."

"Until when?" Mrs. Frankl asked gently.

"Until this morning. Maybe yesterday. Maybe last night in the parlor when I finally admitted what I was afraid to want." Ella's voice cracked. "I wasted so much time being afraid, being practical, choosing the safe path over the right one."

"The right path isn't always visible from the beginning," Mrs. Frankl said, beginning to measure tea leaves with the precision of a pharmacist. "Sometimes you have to walk the wrong path far enough to recognize the right one when you see it."

She selected three jars—Coming Home, Courage,

and one labeled "Trust in Magic"—blending their contents with movements that spoke of decades of practice. The scent that rose from the mixture was complex, layered, carrying notes of jasmine and cinnamon and something indefinable that tasted like safety.

"Each blend serves a purpose," Mrs. Frankl continued as she worked. "But the secret isn't in the proportions or the exotic ingredients. The secret is in the intention. In understanding that every cup of tea is a conversation between what was and what could be."

"Between the person pouring and the person receiving."

"You remembered! Yes. Between past pain and future possibility. Between the heart that's ready to heal and the heart that's ready to soar." Mrs. Frankl poured steaming water over the blended leaves, and the kitchen filled with steam that seemed to carry whispered promises. "The inn just amplifies the conversation."

As the tea steeped, Mrs. Frankl settled onto the stool beside Ella. She poured the tea into delicate, matching white china cups, the liquid a warm amber that caught the morning light like captured sunshine.

"I've learned over the years that every guest who walks through that door is carrying something—grief, hope, fear, love. Our job isn't to fix them. Our job is to create an environment where they can fix themselves."

Ella accepted the cup with trembling hands,

breathing in steam that carried the scent of possibility. She sipped the tea and felt her world tilt.

The flavor was unlike anything she'd ever experienced—intricate, layered, pungent. But more than taste, it carried sensation: a warmth that spread from her chest outward, easing tensions she hadn't realized she was carrying.

"What is this?" she whispered.

"Sarah's final gift to you," Mrs. Frankl said. "Brewed with love and intention and the accumulated wisdom of five generations of women who understood that some choices can't be made with the head. They have to be made with the heart."

As Ella drank, she felt Sarah's presence in the room —not ghostly or mystical, but warm and approving and utterly real. The grandmother who'd waited seventeen years for her return, who'd never stopped believing that love could bridge any distance, that family could survive any misunderstanding.

"I'm scared," Ella admitted. "What if I'm not who the inn thinks I am? What if I can't live up to her legacy? What if I try and fail and disappoint everyone who's counting on me?"

"What if you succeed?" Mrs. Frankl countered gently. "What if you discover that the inn didn't choose you because you were perfect, but because you were exactly what it needed? What if your grandmother knew something you're only beginning to understand?"

Ella's phone buzzed against the counter—a harsh, mechanical sound that seemed profane in the tea-scented sanctuary they'd created. The display showed Bradley's name, along with a text that probably contained arrival details and corporate ultimatums.

She looked at it for a long moment, then picked it up and powered it off completely.

"The inn will handle Mr. Bradley," Mrs. Frankl said calmly. "It's quite good at helping people see what they're trying to destroy."

"You're not worried?"

"I'm too old to waste energy worrying about things I can't control." Mrs. Frankl refilled Ella's cup, the gesture both practical and ceremonial. "But I'm not too old to fight for what matters. And neither are you."

The tea ceremony continued in comfortable silence, each sip carrying Ella deeper into understanding. This wasn't just about choosing between corporate success and small-town life. This was about choosing between the life she'd been told she should want and the life she actually wanted. And actually wanted her back.

The inn hummed around them, walls and floorboards settling into contentment as if they could sense the shift in Ella's heart. Through the windows, the lake sparkled in late-morning light, the dunes rolling golden toward a horizon that no longer looked like an escape route but like a promise of home.

When her cup was empty, Ella felt transformed. Not magically, not impossibly, but deeply and fundamentally changed. The fear was still there—she wasn't naive enough to think courage meant the absence of fear—but it no longer paralyzed her. Instead, it felt like fuel, like the energy she'd need to fight for what mattered.

"What happens now?" she asked.

"Now you show Mr. Bradley the inn at its best," Mrs. Frankl said, rising to clear the tea service with practiced efficiency. "You let it speak for itself. And you trust that some things are too precious to be reduced to quarterly profits."

"And if he doesn't understand?"

Mrs. Frankl's smile was sharp with anticipation. "Then he'll learn what happens when someone tries to take something that people aren't ready to give up."

Ella stood, feeling steadier than she had in days. The inn's future was still uncertain, the corporate pressure still real, but she was no longer facing it alone. She had Mrs. Frankl's wisdom, the housekeeping sisters' fierce loyalty, the accumulated love of five generations of women who'd understood that some things were worth fighting for.

And she had the inn itself—magical, impossible, stubborn inn that had waited seventeen long for Ella Thompson to find her way back.

She'd chosen her side.

Now it was time to fight for it.

Chapter Thirteen

Liam had driven to the inn Tuesday afternoon with the excuse of checking storm damage, but the truth was simpler and more complicated: he couldn't stay away when Ella was facing whatever corporate wolf was being sent to devour her sanctuary.

The parking lot told the story before he'd even cut the engine. Ella's battered Focus sat in its usual spot, but now it was joined by a sleek black rental sedan that screamed expense account. Working-class practicality next to corporate aggression. David parked beside Goliath.

As he reached for his tools from the truck bed, and then thought better of it, Liam caught sight of movement through the inn's tall windows. Ella, moving through the lobby with a purposefulness he hadn't seen before. Not the frantic energy of Monday's stress-cleaning, but something calmer, more centered. She wore one of her city blazers over dark jeans, Sarah's cardigan nowhere in sight, her hair pulled back in a neat bun with not one loose curl.

She looked like someone who'd made a decision and was prepared to live with the consequences.

Liam felt something shift in his chest, a pride so fierce it almost took his breath away. This was the woman he'd glimpsed in fragments over the past week—confident, purposeful, ready to fight for what mattered. The corporate shell she'd worn like armor was cracking, revealing someone far more interesting underneath.

Someone worth falling for completely.

The front door opened as he approached, and Mrs. Frankl emerged with the particular smile of someone anticipating entertainment.

"Afternoon, Liam," she said, her voice carrying a note of satisfaction. "Perfect timing."

"Everything all right?"

"Everything's exactly as it should be." Her eyes sparkled with something that might have been mischief. "Though Mr. Patterson might disagree shortly."

Before he could ask what that meant, a voice drifted from inside the inn—male, authoritative, dismissive in the way that immediately set Liam's teeth on edge.

"—really need to maximize the efficiency of this space. The front desk takes up far too much of the lobby's footprint. Something more streamlined, modern, would increase traffic flow and create opportunities for retail displays."

Liam stepped into the lobby and got his first look at Bradley Patterson.

The man was exactly what central casting would order for "Corporate Shark." Expensive charcoal suit, soft Italian leather shoes, a tablet clutched in one manicured hand and a laser measuring device in the other. He moved through the lobby like he already owned it, measuring, photographing, reducing everything to data points.

Ella stood near the sand globe, her posture perfect and her expression professionally pleasant. But Liam knew her well enough now to see the signs of controlled anger—the slight tension in her shoulders, the way her hands held perfectly still instead of gesturing as they normally would.

"The decorative elements will obviously need updating," Bradley continued, gesturing dismissively at the sand globe. "This thing's taking up prime real estate that could be used for a concierge station or gift shop display."

"The sand globe is original to the inn," Ella said

calmly. "It's been here for over a century. Guests specifi-cally mention it in their reviews."

"Sentiment doesn't pay dividends, Ella." Bradley's tone was condescending, the voice of someone explaining obvious truths to a slow student. "Our market research shows that boutique travelers want Instagram-worthy experiences, not dusty antiques. We'll commission something more photogenic, more on-brand."

Liam felt his hands curl into fists.

"Of course," Ella replied smoothly. "Though I should mention that our current guest satisfaction ratings are consistently above ninety percent. Revenue has increased twelve percent year-over-year despite the challenging economic climate."

Good girl, Liam thought. Fight with their own weapons.

"Imagine what we could do with proper manage-ment," Bradley said, making notes on his tablet. "Pinna-cle's projections show a potential three-hundred-percent increase in profitability within eighteen months. New marketing, streamlined operations, branded amenities packages."

He moved toward the stairs, and Ella followed with Mrs. Frankl beside her like a battle-tested sergeant. Liam hesitated, then decided storm damage inspection could reasonably include checking the upper floors for water leaks.

The second floor tour was excruciating. Bradley measured everything with mechanical precision, criticizing the "inefficient" room layouts, the "dated" décor, the "wasted space" of reading nooks and window seats. He photographed everything with the cold efficiency of someone cataloguing acquisitions.

"The rooms are too large," he declared, standing in the Rose Suite's doorway. "We could easily subdivide these spaces, increase capacity by forty percent. Maybe add some connecting rooms for families."

"The rooms are sized for comfort and intimacy," Ella countered. "Our guests consistently praise the spaciousness, the ability to truly relax."

"Relaxation is a luxury modern travelers can't afford to pay for." Bradley stepped into the Rose Suite, and Liam could swear the temperature dropped five degrees. "They want efficiency, connectivity, turnover. Romance is nice for marketing copy, but square footage pays the bills."

That's when the door decided to stick.

Bradley twisted the handle, pushed, then pulled. Nothing. The door that had opened smoothly moments before now refused to budge, trapping him in the Rose Suite while Ella, Mrs. Frankl, and Liam stood in the hallway.

"Excuse me," Bradley called, irritation creeping into his professional tone. "The door seems to be—" He pushed harder. "This is ridiculous. It's a simple mechanical function."

Liam stepped forward, hiding his smile. "Sometimes the old doors need a gentle touch. Let me—"

"I don't need help from the local handyman," Bradley snapped. "It's a door, not rocket science."

The words landed like a slap. Local handyman. Dismissive, diminishing, designed to put Liam in his place as someone whose opinion didn't matter, whose presence was barely tolerated.

Liam felt heat rise in his chest, the same protective fury that had gotten him into trouble in high school when tourists made jokes about small-town hicks. But before he could respond, Ella's voice cut through the tension like a blade.

"Mr. Carter is a certified contractor and historic preservation specialist," she said, her tone diamond-sharp. "He's maintained this property for over a decade. His expertise is invaluable."

Liam's hand went to his chest. She'd stood up for him without hesitation, claimed his value when this Chicago hack had tried to diminish it. Something dangerous and wonderful unfurled inside of him.

"Fine," Bradley said, his voice muffled by the still-stuck door. "Just get me out of here. This place has more mechanical problems than a third-world hotel."

Liam approached the door, pressing his palm flat against the wood. The Rose Suite hummed under his touch, vibrating with the particular energy that meant the inn was paying attention.

"Easy," he murmured, too quietly for Bradley to hear. "Let him go. He's not worth it."

The door swung open so suddenly that Bradley stumbled backward, catching himself against the dresser with a curse that would have made the housekeeping sisters wash his mouth with soap.

"Old building," Liam said mildly. "Sometimes they have opinions."

Bradley straightened his tie with shaking hands. "This entire property needs updating. The mechanical systems are clearly unreliable, the infrastructure outdated. It'll require significant investment to bring it up to contemporary hospitality standards."

"Or," Mrs. Frankl said quietly, "it requires people who understand how to work with it rather than against it."

Bradley's laugh was sharp and humorless. "Buildings don't have personalities, ma'am. They have structural integrity and market value. Everything else is projection and wishful thinking."

The inn's response was immediate and unmistakable. Every door on the second floor slammed shut simultaneously—not violently, but with enough force and coordination to make a point. The sound echoed through the hallway like a gunshot, followed by absolute silence.

Bradley went pale. "That was... the wind. Pressure differential from the storm damage."

"Of course," Ella agreed pleasantly. "Though there's no wind today. And all the windows are closed."

The tour continued to the third floor, where Bradley's frustration mounted with each "malfunction." His measuring device kept displaying error messages. His phone couldn't maintain a signal. The elevator, when he tried to use it, stopped between floors for exactly thirty seconds before continuing—just long enough to make him sweat.

"This place is falling apart," he declared, emerging from the elevator with his perfect hair slightly mussed. "The systems failures alone would justify a complete renovation. Strip it down to the bones, rebuild with modern efficiency."

"Strip it down," Ella repeated, and Liam heard something new in her voice—steel wrapped in silk. "Eliminate everything that makes it unique."

"Unique doesn't scale, Ella. Unique doesn't generate sustainable revenue streams." Bradley was warming to his theme now, the corporate evangelist spreading the gospel of profit margins. "What you call character, I call inefficiency. What you call charm, I call missed opportunities."

They'd reached the Stargazer Suite, where Arthur Pemberton was presumably taking his afternoon rest. Bradley approached the door with his measuring tape extended, ready to reduce the circular room to square footage calculations.

"I should mention," Ella said quietly, "we have a guest—"

"Who'll need to be relocated during renovation anyway." Bradley knocked briskly on the door. "Sir? Mr. Pemberton? I need to take some measurements for our assessment."

No answer came from within, though Liam could swear he heard the soft sound of pages turning. Arthur was probably reading by the window, lost in memories of Eleanor.

Bradley knocked again, harder. "Sir? This will only take a moment."

When still no answer came, he tried the handle. Like the Rose Suite, the door refused to budge.

"Piece of junk," Bradley muttered, putting his shoulder against the wood. "What is it with the doors in this place?"

"Perhaps Mr. Pemberton is sleeping," Mrs. Frankl

suggested. "He's here for a very personal reason. It would be kind to let him rest."

"Kind doesn't pay operating expenses," Bradley snapped, then caught himself and forced his professional smile back into place. "I'm sure he'll understand. This is business."

He knocked again, loud enough to wake the dead. "Mr. Pemberton! I really do need access to this room!"

That's when Liam reached his limit.

Maybe it was the casual dismissal of Arthur's grief. Maybe it was the systematic destruction of everything the inn represented. Maybe it was the way Bradley talked to Ella like she was an inconvenience rather than someone fighting for her heritage.

Or maybe it was simpler than that. Maybe it was the way Ella stood straighter every time Bradley insulted something she loved, the way she'd defended Liam without hesitation, the way she was learning to fight for what mattered even when the cost was everything she'd built in her old life.

Maybe it was that he'd fallen completely, irrevocably in love with a woman who was brave enough to give up a decent career and take a risk on an inn that defied explanation, and he'd be damned if he'd watch some corporate shark tear apart her dreams.

"That's enough," Liam said, his voice carrying the

quiet authority that had stopped bar fights and settled neighborhood disputes for over a decade.

Bradley turned, eyebrows raised in surprise that the local handyman had dared to speak. "Excuse me?"

"I said that's enough. Mr. Pemberton lost his wife eight months ago. He's here to honor her memory, to find some peace. You banging on his door like a debt collector isn't business—it's cruelty."

"I don't need lessons in customer service from—"

"From someone who actually knows these people?" Liam stepped closer, using his height advantage without being overtly threatening. "You've been here two hours and you've dismissed everything that makes this inn special. The history, the community, the way it actually helps people heal. You see problems where everyone else sees character."

Bradley's round face flushed red. "I see revenue potential being wasted on sentiment. This property could generate three times its current income with proper management and strategic renovation."

"By gutting everything that makes it worth visiting in the first place."

"By bringing it into the twenty-first century!" Bradley's professional mask was slipping, revealing the frustrated aggression underneath. "Look, I don't expect someone like you to understand market dynamics or hospitality trends. This is complex business analysis—"

"Someone like me," Liam repeated, his voice deadly quiet.

Beside him, Ella went very still. Mrs. Frankl's eyes sharpened with interest. Even the inn seemed to hold its breath.

"I only meant—" Bradley started, then stopped, realizing he'd stepped into something deeper than professional disagreement.

"You meant someone who lives here. Someone who works with his hands. Someone who chooses community over profit." Liam's smile held no warmth. "Someone whose opinion doesn't matter because I'm not wearing a suit that costs more than most people make in a month."

"That's not what I—"

"It's exactly what you meant." Liam took another step forward, and Bradley backed up instinctively. "You've spent all this time telling us everything that's wrong with this place, but you haven't asked a single question about why it works. Why people drive from three states away to stay here. Why couples get engaged in the garden and come back for their anniversaries twenty years later. Why Arthur Pemberton couldn't bear to miss his wife's birthday tradition even though it breaks his heart to be here without her."

Bradley's mouth opened and closed soundlessly.

"You want to know what I see?" Liam continued,

his voice carrying the certainty of someone who'd found his cause worth fighting for. "I see a place that's been healing hearts for over a century. I see a woman who's brave enough to choose love over security, magic over money. I see something worth protecting from people who think everything valuable can be reduced to a spreadsheet."

"Ridiculous," Bradley sputtered, but his voice had lost its authority. "You're talking about fantasy, not business reality. Buildings don't heal hearts. Properties don't perform magic. This is all just... projection and wishful thinking."

The words hung in the air like a challenge thrown down.

And the inn answered.

The elevator cables screamed as the car plummeted past the third floor—not dangerously, but loud enough to make everyone's hearts skip. The lights flickered in sequence down the hallway, each fixture dimming and brightening like a wave rolling through the building. Deep in the walls came a sound like singing—not quite human, not quite wind, but unmistakably alive.

Bradley went white as paper.

"Old wiring," Mrs. Frankl said blandly. "Very temperamental."

"I need to..." Bradley swallowed hard, looking around the hallway like he expected the walls to start closing in. "I need to finish my assessment. This is a professional evaluation, not some... supernatural tourist trap."

But his hands shook as he made notes on his tablet, and he kept glancing over his shoulder like he expected something to follow him.

The tour concluded in the lobby, where Bradley tried to regain his composure by focusing on concrete details—square footage, traffic patterns, revenue optimization. But every time he touched something, it seemed to resist him. His measuring tape jammed. His phone displayed error messages. Even his pen ran out of ink mid-sentence.

"This place has serious infrastructure issues," he declared, more to himself than anyone else. "Electrical problems, mechanical failures, obvious maintenance concerns. The renovation costs alone would be substantial."

"I don't think it's worth it," Ella said. "For Pinnacle."

Bradley looked at her like she'd suggested he try alchemy. "Ella, you're obviously emotionally attached to this property. I understand that. But emotion is the enemy of sound business decisions. Pinnacle can transform this place into something profitable, sustainable, marketable to contemporary consumers."

"By destroying everything that makes it special."

"By recognizing that special doesn't pay bills!" Bradley's frustration finally boiled over, his professional facade cracking completely. "You've let sentiment cloud your judgment. This place is quaint, I'll give you that. Charming in a throwback, nostalgic way. But charm doesn't generate revenue growth. Character doesn't drive occupancy rates. And whatever... atmosphere... this place has, it can't compete with modern amenities and professional management."

"You're wrong," Ella said, and her voice carried a certainty that made Liam's chest swell with pride. "The inn makes a profit month after month, year after year."

"One percent! And you're going to keep it going. Ella, I know you're capable, but this? This is impossible."

I'm offering you a way out of an impossible situation," Bradley continued. "A way to salvage your career, your financial future, your professional reputation. Pinnacle's offer is generous, the timeline is reasonable, and the commission would set you up for years."

"The inn isn't for sale."

The words fell into the lobby like stones into still water, creating ripples that seemed to spread through the very air. The sand globe on its pedestal began to swirl, golden sand forming spirals that caught the afternoon light like tiny galaxies.

Bradley stared at her. "What did you say?"

"I said the Starlight Arbor Inn is not for sale to Pinnacle Hospitality." Ella's voice was calm, professional, and absolutely final. "Not now, not ever."

"Ella, you can't be serious. You're throwing away your career over a building that's held together by wishful thinking and prayer. When Markie finds out—"

"Then I guess I'm choosing a different career."

The simple statement hit the lobby like a thunderclap. Liam felt his heart stop, restart, then begin beating double-time as the full implications crashed over him.

She'd chosen. Not just the inn, not just the magic, but the life that came with them. The community, the responsibility, the uncertain future that required faith instead of quarterly projections.

She'd chosen them.

Chosen him.

Bradley's face cycled through disbelief, anger, and finally a cold professionalism that was somehow more threatening than his earlier bluster.

"You'll regret this," he said, his voice carrying the particular certainty of someone who'd never been wrong about human weakness. "When the romance wears off and you're struggling to make payroll, when you realize that good intentions don't pay property taxes or insurance premiums, when the reality of running a failing business crashes down on your head—you'll remember this conversation."

"Maybe," Ella agreed pleasantly. "But I'll remember it as the day I chose what mattered over what was easy."

"And on that day," Bradley continued, "we'll be back. Offering half what we'd get today. One-quarter."

As Bradley stalked toward the door, the inn delivered its final judgment. The elevator cables screamed again, so loud and sudden that Bradley jumped like he'd been electrocuted. Every door in the building slammed shut simultaneously—guest rooms, closets, the front entrance itself—creating a percussion that reverberated through the walls like a giant's heartbeat.

Only the main entrance remained open.

Bradley ran.

Actually ran, his expensive shoes slapping on the porch, on the sidewalk as he fled toward his rental car. Through the windows, they watched him fumble with his keys, drop his tablet, nearly fall trying to get the door open. The engine turned over on the third try, and he reversed out of the parking lot fast enough to spray gravel across the lawn.

In the sudden quiet that followed his departure, Liam became acutely aware that he was alone with Ella in the lobby, Mrs. Frankl having discreetly vanished during the final confrontation.

"So," he said, voice rough with emotions he was afraid to name. "You chose."

"I chose," she confirmed, and when she turned to

face him, her eyes were bright with unshed tears and determination and something that made his heart skip. "I chose this place. This life. This…" She gestured between them. "Whatever this is."

"This," Liam said, stepping closer until he could see the gold flecks in her eyes, smell the vanilla and jasmine scent that was becoming as necessary as breathing, "is me falling in love with the bravest woman I've ever met."

Her breath caught. "Liam—"

"This is me watching you stand up to a corporate shark and choose magic over money, community over career, faith over security." He reached up to cup her face, thumb brushing across her cheekbone. "This is me realizing that I've been waiting my whole life for someone like you to come home."

She leaned into his touch, eyes fluttering closed. "I'm scared," she whispered. "I just threw away everything I built, everything I worked for. I have no idea how to run this place, how to keep it profitable, how to—"

"Hey." He waited until she opened her eyes, met his gaze. "You're not doing this alone. You've got Mrs. Frankl, the sisters, everybody in town pulling for you. You've got me, if you'll have me."

"Are you sure?" Her voice was small, vulnerable in a way that made his chest ache. "I'm not the successful corporate woman anymore. I'm just someone who owns an inn she doesn't know how to run, who threw away her career for something she can't even explain."

"You're someone who saw what mattered and fought for it," he said, leaning down until their foreheads touched. "You're someone who chose love over fear, magic over logic, belonging over success. You're exactly who I hoped you'd turn out to be."

The kiss that followed was gentle, tentative, full of promise and possibility and the sweetness of two people who'd found something worth fighting for.

Around them, the inn seemed to sigh with contentment, the sand globe's golden spirals catching the light like tiny stars being born.

When they broke apart, Ella was smiling through her tears.

"What happens now?" she asked.

"Now," Liam said, pulling her closer until she fit against his chest like she'd been designed to be there, "we figure it out. Together."

"Together," she repeated, testing the word like it was foreign but wonderful.

Outside, storm clouds were gathering again over Lake Michigan, but inside the Starlight Arbor Inn, everything was exactly as it should be.

Chapter Fourteen

The library had always been Liam's favorite room in the inn, though he'd never been able to articulate exactly why. Now, standing beside Ella in the soft lamplight Tuesday evening, he thought he was beginning to understand.

The room occupied the entire back corner of the second floor, its tall windows facing both the lake and the wooded hills that rolled away toward the heart of Michigan. Floor-to-ceiling bookshelves lined three walls, filled with an eclectic collection that seemed to have grown organically over the decades—leather-bound classics sharing space with paperback mysteries, travel guides next to volumes of poetry, local histories nestled beside philosophy texts.

The air carried scents of old paper, leather, and tea, with an undertone of beeswax from the polished reading lamps positioned throughout the space. A stone fireplace dominated the interior wall, its mantel crowded with framed photographs and small treasures. Two wingback chairs in faded burgundy leather flanked the hearth, positioned to catch both firelight and the last rays of evening sun.

Ella stood near the writing desk in the corner, still wearing the blazer she'd worn for her confrontation with Bradley, though she'd loosened her hair from its severe bun. Chestnut curls fell around her shoulders, catching the lamplight like captured fire. She looked simultaneously exhausted and exhilarated, like someone who'd just survived a battle they'd never expected to win.

"I keep waiting to regret it," she said quietly, not looking at him. "The career, the security, the life I spent six years building. I keep expecting the panic to hit, the realization that I've made a terrible mistake."

"And?" Liam settled into one of the wingback chairs, studying her profile in the golden light.

"And instead I feel..." She paused, searching for the right word. "Free. Terrified, but free. Like I've been holding my breath for years and finally remembered how to exhale."

"You chose what mattered," he said. "That's not something most people have the courage to do."

"I chose the unknown over the secure, magic over logic, a life I don't know how to live over one I'd mastered." She finally turned to face him, and he could see the wonder in her eyes, mixed with excitement—or terror. "I was re-reading Sarah's letter. She left me a key. She said it would open what needed opening when the time was right."

She pulled it out of a pocket in her blazer, holding it up to catch the lamplight. One of those big old-fashioned brass keys, gleaming like captured sunlight. Hooked onto it, a star-shaped charm seemed to pulse with its own inner warmth. "I've been carrying it around for two weeks, waiting to understand what it was for."

"And now?"

"Now I think I'm ready to find out."

The key felt warm in her palm as she stood, heavier than its size suggested. As she moved through the library, it seemed to pull gently in a specific direction—not magnetically, but with the same insistent tug of intuition that had guided her choices all week.

"Every time I came in here, I would remember the key," she said. "It must mean something."

Liam followed as she approached the poetry section. She ran her fingers along the spines of books that had been arranged and rearranged by generations of guests. Shakespeare, Frost, Dickinson, Browning, Khayyám,

Harper. The greatest voices of love and loss and wonder, their words worn soft by countless hands seeking comfort in verse.

"Here," Ella said suddenly, stopping before a leather-bound volume of Shakespeare's sonnets. The book looked older than the others, its spine etched with stars that matched the charm on her key. "It has to be here."

She tried to pull the volume out, but it seemed stuck. Instead, she pressed gently against the book's spine, and it depressed like a button with a soft click.

The entire section of shelving swung inward, revealing a narrow doorway and a flight of stairs leading upward into darkness.

"Impossible," Liam breathed, though by now he should have learned to stop saying that word around the inn.

"Come with?" Ella said.

The stairs were narrow and steep, carved from the same dark wood as the library shelves. They climbed in a tight spiral, and Liam found himself counting steps—thirteen, fourteen, fifteen—before they reached a landing that shouldn't have been able to exist within the inn's architecture.

A heavy wooden door waited at the top, its surface carved with the same star patterns they'd seen throughout the inn. The brass lock was shaped like a lynx's head, its gemstone eyes glinting in the dim light that filtered down from somewhere above.

Ella inserted the key with trembling fingers. The lock turned with a sound like wind chimes. The door swung open on silent hinges, releasing a breath of air that smelled of starlight and secrets.

The room beyond defied every law of physics and architecture Liam thought he understood.

It was circular, maybe twenty feet across, with a domed ceiling that rose higher than should have been possible given the inn's structure. The walls were lined with windows—tall, narrow, multi-paned windows that offered views of Green Arbor, the lake, and the surrounding countryside that were far too expansive for a room tucked between the second and third floors.

Through the windows, the inn's own grounds spread like an well-mown apron, but also the town center, the lighthouse on the distant shore, the rolling dunes that stretched toward the horizon. It was as if the room sat atop a tower that existed in its own dimensional space, offering a view of the entire world the inn protected.

"How is this possible?" he asked, though his voice held awe rather than skepticism.

"Magic," Ella said simply, moving into the room

with the careful steps of someone entering a cathedral. "Real, undeniable, impossible magic."

The room was furnished like a scholar's study crossed with an astronomer's observatory. A large round oak desk dominated the center, its surface covered with maps, charts, and leather-bound journals. Bookshelves lined the spaces between windows, filled with volumes that looked older than the inn itself. A brass telescope stood near the eastern window, pointed toward the dunes where legend said the lynx had made its sacrifice.

But it was the maps that drew Liam's attention. Spread across the desk and pinned to every available wall surface, they showed Green Arbor and the surrounding region in detail he'd never seen. Not just the physical geography, but something else—lines of energy that flowed like invisible rivers through the landscape, connecting the inn to specific locations throughout the area.

"Ley lines," Ella said, following his gaze. "Channels of energy that flow through the land, concentrating at specific points." She traced one of the lines with her finger, following its path from the inn to the lighthouse, then to the dunes, then to other locations marked with symbols he didn't recognize. "Each room in the inn is connected to a different line, a different type of energy."

Liam leaned over the desk, studying the intricate network of lines and symbols. The maps were hand-drawn, clearly the work of many years, with notes and corrections in multiple handwritings. Some were in Sarah's careful script, others in hands that looked much older.

"The Lighthouse Keeper's Room," he read from one notation, "draws on the energy of guidance and safe harbor. The Rose Suite channels love and second chances. The Stargazer Suite connects to destiny and divine timing." He looked up at Ella. "This is how the inn knows what people need. It's not random magic—it's a system."

"A system that requires someone to tend it," Ella said, lifting a leather journal from the desk. The cover was embossed with the same star pattern they'd seen throughout the room, and the pages inside were filled with careful observations in Sarah's handwriting. "Listen to this: 'The inn doesn't create magic—it focuses and channels energy that already exists in the land. The innkeeper's role is to serve as a conduit, helping to direct that energy where it's needed most.'"

She turned pages, reading passages that documented decades of careful observation: guest arrivals that coincided with specific energy patterns, rooms that seemed to call to certain people, interventions that helped heal hearts and minds in ways that couldn't be explained by conventional hospitality.

"'September 15th, 2019,'" she read aloud. "'Young

couple in the Harbor Master's Room, marriage failing after loss of child. Storm brought them together with elderly widower in Stargazer Suite who shared his story of love surviving grief. Sometimes healing requires witnessing another's strength.' There are hundreds of entries like this, Liam. Decades of Sarah watching, learning, helping."

Liam moved to the eastern window, looking out over the dunes where the lynx legend had begun. The view was impossibly clear, as if he could see for miles despite the growing darkness. "My grandfather knew about this, didn't he?"

"Oh! Read this," Ella said, handing him a folder filled with newspaper clippings, photographs, and handwritten notes. The tab read "Guardian Families" in Sarah's careful script.

Inside, he found documentation going back over a century—records of families who'd served as protectors and helpers for the inn's magic. The Carters featured prominently, with notes about his great-grandfather, grandfather, and father. Men who'd maintained the physical structure while understanding that their real job was protecting something far more precious.

"'The Carter men have always known,'" Ella read from Sarah's notes. "'They understand that some repairs can't be measured with tools, that some maintenance requires heart rather than hands. Each generation produces one who hears the inn's voice, who understands their role as guardian and protector.'"

The folder contained photographs spanning decades—his grandfather as a young man, standing beside Sarah's grandmother. His father helping with renovations in the 1980s. And there, in the most recent photo, himself at nineteen, helping install new gutters while Sarah watched from the porch with a satisfied smile.

"She knew," he said quietly. "Even then, she knew."

"She knew we'd find each other," Ella agreed. "Look at this."

She handed him a sealed envelope with his name written across the front in Sarah's familiar handwriting. Inside, a letter dated only days before Sarah's death:

Dear Liam,

If you're reading this, then Ella has found her courage and you've both discovered what I've known for years—you belong together, not just as lovers but as partners in the inn's sacred work.

Your grandfather understood the burden and the blessing of serving as guardian. It's not an easy path. It requires you to believe in things others might dismiss, to protect something precious without taking credit for its gifts. But it's also the most rewarding work we can do—helping others find their way home to themselves and each other.

Ella will need your strength, your practical wisdom,

your unwavering faith in the impossible. The inn has been waiting for her, but it's also been preparing you. Every repair you've made, every crisis you've helped resolve, every moment you've chosen to stay rather than leave—all of it has been preparation for this.

Trust your instincts. Trust the inn. Trust each other.

With love and gratitude,

Sarah Porter

Liam's throat went tight as he finished reading. The letter made sense of things he'd never understood—his grandfather's stories, his own inability to leave Green Arbor despite opportunities elsewhere, the way he'd always felt connected to the inn in ways that went beyond professional responsibility.

"Guardian," he said, testing the word. "I like the sound of that."

"Partner," Ella corrected gently, moving to stand beside him at the window. "According to these journals, the inn works best when the keeper and guardian work together. Two people who complement each other's strengths, who can handle both the practical and magical aspects of what this place requires."

Outside, the first stars were appearing in the darkening sky, their light reflecting off the lake's surface like scattered diamonds. From their impossible vantage point in the secret room, they could see the entire world they'd committed to protecting—the town, the lake, the dunes where legend said love had triumphed over destruction.

"There's more," Ella said, retrieving another envelope from the desk. This one was addressed simply to "The Next Keeper" in Sarah's careful script.

The letter inside was longer, more detailed, explaining the inn's true purpose and the weight of responsibility that came with accepting its care:

*My dear one,

If you're reading this, you've chosen to accept the role that has been calling to you, perhaps longer than you've realized. The Starlight Arbor Inn is more than a business, more than a building, more than a family legacy. It's a sanctuary for hearts seeking their way home—to love, to healing, to themselves.

The magic isn't in the walls or the furniture or even the land, though all of these serve as conduits. The magic is in the choosing—choosing to believe the impossible, choosing to serve something greater than yourself, choosing to trust that love is stronger than fear, hope more powerful than despair.

Each guest who finds their way here brings a different need, a different wound to heal, a different joy to celebrate. Your job isn't to fix them—it's to provide the space and the subtle guidance that allows them to fix themselves. The inn will help, will offer signs and opportunities, but the real healing happens when people choose to remain open to possibility.

It won't always be easy. There will be days when the responsibility feels overwhelming, when the magic seems more burden than blessing, when you question whether you're strong enough for what this place requires. In those moments, remember that you're not alone. The inn itself will support you, as will the community that depends on what you protect. And if you're blessed as I hope you will be, you'll have a partner who understands both the weight and the joy of this calling.

Trust the inn. Trust your instincts. Trust that love—in all its forms—is worth whatever sacrifice it requires.

All my love and faith,

Sarah Porter*

By the time Ella finished reading, her cheeks were wet with tears. Liam pulled her into his arms, holding her as she cried for the grandmother who'd loved her enough to wait seventeen years for her return, for the weight of responsibility she was accepting, for the life she was choosing over the one she'd planned.

"I'm scared," she whispered against his chest. "What if I'm not strong enough? What if I disappoint her, disappoint everyone who's counting on me?"

"We'll figure it out together," he said, pressing a kiss to the top of her head. "That's what partners do."

They stood together in the secret room as full darkness fell outside, watching the lights of Green Arbor twinkle below like earthbound stars. The inn hummed around them with contentment.

Ella's phone, which had been mercifully quiet since she'd turned it back on after Bradley's departure, suddenly erupted with incoming calls and messages. Markie's name flashed on the screen repeatedly, accompanied by text previews that promised professional devastation and corporate retribution.

"I should probably..." Ella started, then stopped, looking at the phone like it was a snake.

"Face the music?" Liam suggested gently.

She answered on the fourth ring, putting it on speaker so he could hear.

"Ella Thompson, what the hell do you think you're doing?" Markie's voice filled the secret room like toxic smoke, harsh and angry and utterly out of place in the magical sanctuary they'd discovered.

"My job," Ella replied calmly. "As owner of the Starlight Arbor Inn."

"Your job is as a senior associate at Premier Properties, working on the biggest commission of your career! Bradley's report is a disaster—he says you've lost your mind. He says you actually believe the place is haunted!"

"Not haunted," Ella corrected. "Magical. There's a difference."

The silence on the other end of the line stretched

long enough that Liam wondered if the call had dropped. When Markie spoke again, her voice was carefully controlled.

"Ella, I'm going to pretend you didn't just say that. I'm going to assume you're having some kind of breakdown brought on by stress and grief, and I'm going to give you twenty-four hours to come to your senses. Return to Chicago, submit a professional assessment, and let Pinnacle handle the property acquisition like we planned."

"The inn isn't for sale, Markie. Not to Pinnacle, not to anyone."

"Then you're fired." The words came fast and sharp, delivered with the satisfaction of someone who'd been pushed past their limit. "Effective immediately. Clear out your office—no, we'll clear it out. Return your company equipment, and don't expect a reference. You've destroyed your career over a fantasy, Ella. I hope your haunted house keeps you warm when you're broke and unemployed."

"I won't need a reference," Ella responded. "I have a calling."

She ended the call before Markie could respond, then powered off the phone completely.

"Well," she said, looking at Liam with a mixture of terror and exhilaration, "that's that. I'm officially unemployed, unemployable, and committed to a life I have no idea how to live."

"You're officially free," he corrected, pulling her closer. "Free to build something meaningful instead of profitable, something that matters instead of something that just makes money."

"Are you sure about this?" she asked, her hands fisting in his flannel shirt. "About me, about us, about taking on responsibility for an impossible magical inn that requires faith more than business sense?"

"Thompson," he said, his voice rough with emotion and certainty, "you've had me since you stood in that puddle of coffee on your first morning, ready to fight the universe. I've been yours since you accepted Mrs. Henderson's miracle, since you rolled with the tea pot choir, since you had the courage to build a life based on love instead of fear."

"I love you," she whispered, the words carrying the weight of commitment and possibility. "I love you, and I love this place, and I love the life we're going to build together."

"I love you too," he replied, cupping her face in his hands. "I love your courage, your heart, your willingness to choose wonder over safety. I love that you're brave enough to believe in magic, strong enough to fight for what matters."

The kiss that followed was different, and definitely not tentative. Deeper, sure of itself, full of promise and passion and joy of two people who'd found something worth building a life around. Liam never wanted to let her go. Around them, the secret room seemed to pulse with approval, the windows reflecting their joined figures like a benediction.

When they finally broke apart, both breathing hard, the inn had settled into a contented hum that vibrated through the walls and floor.

"What happens now?" Ella asked, still in his arms, looking around the room that held the secrets of her inheritance and her future.

"Now," Liam said, pressing his forehead against hers, "we go downstairs and see what the inn thinks of our partnership. And then we start figuring out how to serve something bigger than ourselves."

"Together," she said, and it wasn't a question.

"Together," he confirmed, sealing the promise with another kiss. She felt great, smelled better, and tasted perfect.

As they made their way back down the secret stairs, hand in hand, the inn welcomed them with golden light and the sense of pieces finally falling into place. When they reached the lobby, the sand globe swirled with new intensity, showing visions of the inn through seasons yet to come—guests finding healing, love being celebrated, hearts discovering what they'd thought they'd lost forever.

And in the middle of it all, two figures working side by side, tending the magic that connected heaven and earth, helping others find their way home to themselves and each other.

The Starlight Arbor Inn had found its keeper and its guardian.

Now the real magic could begin.

Also by Annika Stone

Green Arbor Stories

Room for Magic

Room for Light

Room for Dreams

The Room for Magic Trilogy

Sweet Romance

The Author Next Door

A Taste of Tradition

Lilac Hearts

A Melody for Sunshine

Level Up to Love

Cosmic Hearts

Wild Hearts of Yellowstone

The Christmas Cookie Trap

Winter's Gift

The Valentine's Ruse

About the Author

Annika Stone writes sweet contemporary romance where love shows up in unexpected places—small towns, big cities, magical inns, or ordinary Tuesdays. Her characters are everyday people with interesting lives, real problems, and hearts that recognize home when they find it. She's eternally hopeful, perpetually daydreaming, and absolutely certain everyone deserves their happy ending.

www.ingramcontent.com/pod-product-compliance
Lightning Source LLC
Chambersburg PA
CBHW060539190726
48283CB00003B/794